OYABIYI OBASEGUN AJINAKU

OBA

The Rise of a True King

A NOVEL

To A Forgotten Era.

Okan

A game of ayo occupied Arèmo Bode's mind while he waited for his brother's birth outside his parent's bedroom. The young prince's fingers moved marbles from one hole to another as everyone moved excitedly throughout the aafin. Months turned into hours as Bode made one last prayer for solidarity in his mother's eyes.

One of the king's servants stormed from the room and yelled, "Ẹso, fetch Oju now!"

The guard sitting with Bode jumped from the plush, red stool and flew down the hall. Bode smiled. He thought his prayers were answered.

Oju appeared in the hall, his garb flowed with his swift walk. He carried a small, black pouch as twelve of his students followed him, as well as, the guard stringing along six rams. The rams' left eyes settled on Bode. He sliced a shiny red apple as he watched the wind press against the white beards. The last ram stopped to enjoy the tasty crescent offer Bode tossed.

As the guard crossed the threshold he jolted backwards. "Wa!" the guard yelled as he turned to see why the rams stopped. "Come!" he said as he yanked the rope to pull the rams into the room.

Bode stood up to catch a glimpse of the unusual occasion. Chubby, small legs sprang from his mother as his father sweated profusely. Heat waves rose from the cloth his father wrung out over a small, white bowl before he dabbed his mother's forehead. Bode's eyes weren't keen enough to see the old woman, Iyalase, dressed in a white lapa with red stitching. She stood next to his mother. She frowned as she watched the peeking Bode smirk. Her eyes, the doorway into the beginning of time, made everyone, even the Gods themselves, humbly bow. If the people in the room saw her, they'd bow too while holding their breath until the Elder Mother spoke. Bode only looked into the room for a few seconds before the doors closed in front of him.

Oju, the oba's most trusted Babaláwo, as well as

the high priest of the Sango Temple in the kingdom of Jefe, held a turtle shell opele in the air. In his other hand he held a small blade with an ivory carved handle. He saw the old woman that represented the Íyami, the Scared Mothers of the Universe. He knew Iyalase was there to watch this event as they watch everything else. Oju cast his opele twice to see if he may proceed with the ritual. He could.

A thunderous movement crept up the aafin's walls. Oju saw streaks of lightning outside the window as his enchanting timber rose. Frighten rams stomped their hooves before pairs of Oju's students picked them up one by one. They let out a shrieking cry before Oju pierced their throats with the blade's tip. Blood rained into the calabash holding a large, black stone.

Oba Kola listened to Ife scream not from pain, but out of fear for their second born. He watched Oju slit every ram's throat as the midwife pulled his son out of Ife. Oju grabbed the baby from the midwife's arms. He unwrapped the umbilical cord tied around the newborn's neck. Everyone stood silent as they listened for the newborn's first cries. The baby was breathless. Oju dipped the blade's tip in the calabash and marked a thunderbolt symbol in blood on the newborn's forehead. In the baby's left ear his whispers rang like a song.

A gust of wind, followed by the heaven's roar, wafted through the window as Oju finished reciting to the lifeless newborn. A stroke of wind brushed past Oju's face touching the baby's paling lips. The small belly rose and when it lowered the screeching cry pleased all the ears within the room.

Oju sang aloud to the king of heaven, Sango. As he sang he held the newborn over the calabash and with a cup bathed him in blood. After Oju cleaned the child with an herbal elixir, he past him to the midwife who wrapped the baby in cloth before passing him to his father's outstretched arms. Oba Kola passed the baby to Ife. His forehead laid on hers as he watched her tears splatter off the baby's face.

Oju leaned towards the king's ear. "When he's older my friend, he must be initiated so that he may have a long life," he whispered. "Sango has claimed him."

Oju instructed his students to clean the space as he sat on a mat to cast his opele. "Ohun gbogbo daradara," Oju exclaimed as he clapped his hands. "Everything's well."

He searched the room for Iyalase. His eyes set on a pearl white bird with red and black stripe feather tips sitting on a branch outside the window, untouched by rain. His many years of training taught him it was Iyalase.

Outside the room, anger flushed Bode's as he swiped the ayo board. Each piece clamored on the marble floor. In his hand, Bode held a clay king figurine he bought from an elderly woman in the market. He crushed it in his palm. Red droplets of blood struck the floor near his feet.

Oba Kola burst from the room to find his first born son. "Bode." He ran to his son placing his palms on Bode's shoulders. "You have a brother." He waited for Bode to smile with him. "What's wrong?" Oba Kola's hands slid down Bode's arms to lock hands. He felt moisture. "Are you hurt?" He opened Bode's hands to find pieces of clay sticking out of his palms. He looked closer and found a crown.

Oba Kola pondered that day as orange embers burned while he waited in his golden fleece robe. He sat on a jade stool drinking out of an emerald studded cup. His eyebrows furrowed as his plump cheeks hung in an ever concerned frown. His kingdom was flourishing with trade along the river, but darkness loomed within the aafin. Ife was gone for quite some time now. She fell to a plague because her family failed to meet an obligations to the God of Earth, Obaluaiye, when she was born.

Oba Kola had other wives but his first wife, Ife, was his joy. She balanced him. She taught him to rule with a just consciousness. Anyone she met she greeted with a smile and a joke to break the tension of being in royalty's presence. The people liked Oba Kola because of her. It was Ife who bore the heir to his throne.

Before Bode's birth, the young Oba Kola was

obsessed with empire expansion, pushing the Jama further North. On Bode's birth day, a war brewed in the North. Time forced Oba Kola to leave his wife's side. "Within seven days I'll return a victor," he arrogantly told his wife as he rode away on his black stallion followed by a myriad of men. Within seven days he solemnly returned, a piece of his kingdom lost with over half the Jefe Army to the Jama sword before retreating. Losing many wars thereafter encouraged him to place his faith of redemption on Bode's shoulders. He prayed his son never saw defeat and his kingdom never lost its religious values like the Hausa and Fulani who turned Jihadist.

Ife later told Oba Kola the labor was torturous, "like the baby was cutting his way out." Realizing Bode's fire lead to a potent warrior, Oba Kola provided a stimulating environment by keeping him around skilled ęso and bringing him along to small scrimmage battles.

At young age, Bode mastered tactics. He even became adept at ayo, often beating Oba Kola. As Bode grew into young manhood, his skills in weaponry, fighting and military stratagem predicted Jefe's blossom. Ife became worried when Bode plunged a knife into one of his servants, ripping the intestines out to play in blood. Still controlled by greed, Oba Kola turned a blind eye to many of these occurrences. He fed Bode's thirst by keeping him in battle zones, appointing him his second-in-command general. Ife, on the other hand, attempted to turn Bode from his vicious acts. She failed. Her next pregnancy she focused on a child full of light.

Eventually, overbearing reports of Bode's wickedness in battle and at home caused Oba Kola to question his judgement. After his upset grandfather visited him in a dream, Oba Kola aimed for a kingdom of peace and prosperity. Changing his tactics made the kingdom thrive. It also confused the war hungry Bode leaving him with very little purpose.

During this growth Oba Kola came to love his second son more. He saw Ife every time he looked into Sakin's eyes. Oba Kola saw Sakin's wisdom, clever mili-

tary tactics and his love for the people. He saw the king
he wished to Bode would become. Whenever Sakin
was around Ife was lighter, smiling and laughing more.
She seemed cold when Sakin was sent away to be initiated by Oju. Bode couldn't please her with his brute
temperament and embittering slurs to the servants.

With each passing day Oba Kola's muscles became fragile. His hair snowed atop his wrinkling face
with skin the texture of a muddied elephant. Oba Kola
walked with the same royal staff his father and grandfather walked with, a tale of age. Each day he grew tired
of listening to villagers' arguments about land, business men rift with tariffs, threats of Jama attacks in the
North and jealousy among his wives. Oba Kola needed
to meet with Oju as the night yawned.

Three knocks pounded against the door of his
chambers.

"Oba," a guard said as he entered. "Oju has arrived."

Oju entered with a glistening smile. "Ore mi,"
he said as he walked towards the open stool to sit. "My

friend."

"You may leave us." Oba Kola watched the guard walk backwards to leave.

"Your spirits are down. Why have you sent for me so late in the evening?"

"May I offer you some wine?" Oba Kola poured some wine in a small cup after Oju nodded.

"What troubles you?" Oju asked before he sipped his drink.

"It has been a long time since I've sent for you in this manner."

"Yes, the kingdom has been peaceful. And Sakin? Is he well? I haven't seen him for some time now," Oju smiled.

"Bẹẹni." Oba Kola half way smiled as he thought about his beloved son.

Oba Kola sipped wine before he addressed his deep concern. "My diviners have carried me through while you were away in your travels. I feel they've been compromised. I need you." Oba Kola stared at the embers as if he were listening for the answers he already knew. "I want to know what'll happen to my kingdom when I die."

Oju looked at his friend sternly as he placed his cup down. He opened his bag to grab his Elegba shrine, mat and opele. As Oju sang his incantations to hearken the ears of the Gods, thunder rolled softly throughout Jefe. Then the earth shook as boulders struck each other in heaven, igniting fire in the sky. The two legs of Oju's opele swayed in the air before he pumped his fist away and back to the drop the chain on the mat. Crystals of sweat formed along Oju's brow as he read the sign that fell before him. He immediately swiped his hands over the chain to erase the configuration he saw. His eyes met Oba Kola who asked. "What does it say?"

A split calabash can be mended.

One who spits fire burns everything.

The patient one gets to the end of a troubling road.

Meji

Sakin scarcely visited his father after his mother's death. He spent long periods traveling as his father's emissary or at the Sango Temple. When he did visit his ailing father, he wouldn't leave his side. They talked about the many things happening throughout the kingdom or in the aafin. Oba Kola always had a new story of how his wives plotted against each other to win favor in his eyes or something funny one of his younger children did as they explored life. Sakin talked about familial alliances throughout Jefe and successful rites of passages in various villages. From time to time Sakin came across a yuvo interested in setting up churches within different villages. The villagers declined the offers just like Sakin instructed. To ward off the new visitors they built bigger shrines to sit at the entrance of their village. Oba Kola felt Sakin managed kingdom affairs well outside the capital city.

Arèmo Bode visited Oba Kola less even though he was nearby. Excuses of dealing with subjects or townspeople developed as his movements became more secretive. He denied his father and brother any of his spare time. Both were surprised when Bode followed a servant into the room after they shared their morning meal. The servant grabbed the bowls and exited the room.

"Brother, how good of you to join us," Sakin said as he rose to greet Bode. "It'll be good for all of us to sit and talk," he smiled.

Contempt eclipsed Bode's face once his eyes settled on his younger brother. "I wish to speak with baba alone." He stepped backwards to evade Sakin's embrace.

"But, it's such as rare occasion to have us all in the same room."

"I have business to discuss."

Oba Kola coughed as he sat up in the bed. Sakin walked over to grab pillows to support his father's back. He grabbed a cup of tea for Oba Kola to sip. Leaves swirled as Oba Kola placed the small cup to his lips. The leaves tickled his throat as he swallowed. His cough calmed.

"Sakin, it's fine," Oba Kola said.

Sakin sat the cup down on the bedside table. He felt his brother's cutting glare. Bode balled his fists at his side with his feet together as if commanding an army.

"Ok baba. Is there anything you'd like me to get you?" Sakin asked as he wiped his hands on his buba. While waiting for his father to respond Sakin grabbed his fila and twisted the fabric.

"Bẹẹni. Go to the market and pick us up some opah. Your mother loved that fish," Oba Kola smiled. "I'd like some for lunch."

"Don't we have opah here?"

"I'm sure we do. But, I'd like it as fresh as possible. Our fishermen are just getting back from the river and heading to the marketplace."

Sakin nodded at his father's request and turned to walk away. His father's weak grasp on his forearm stopped him.

"Mo nife o omo mi," Oba Kola said as he squeezed Sakin's hand.

"I love you too, baba." Sakin returned the gesture.

A cold drift hit Sakin as he walked pass his brother. "Take care of baba before I return. Maybe then business'll be finished and we can all have lunch together," Sakin suggested as he turned to leave. "If I remember you enjoy opah too."

Bode stood silently as he looked pass Sakin as Sakin walked by. He waited for the door to close behind him. Once he heard it shut he walked towards his father's bedside.

"Please, sit Bode. It's rare I get to see you these days." Oba Kola waved at the chair by his bed. "Too busy to check up on me I suppose. What troubles you in Jefe today?"

Bode ignored the seat his father suggested as he towered the man in bed. "Baba, there's a town in the West I want to discuss," he said. "I'm going to take it."

"I asked you to sit," Oba Kola croaky voice lowered with abhorrence. Bode walked around the bed and sat in the chair. "There, that's better." He watched his eldest son's tall and beefy physique fill the seat. "Why do you want to take this town? What asset do they prove?"

"The people can be sold. Ships are docking west taking slaves to a new land. It has proven profitable for other kings. I don't see why we'd be any different. The town is closer to the shore so a quick exchange can be made."

Oba Kola shook his head. "We don't take slaves, Bode. We make citizens. Your great-grandfather admonishes against that sort of thing."

"That was then when you and your fathers ruled. Times has changed. More money can be made like this to finance the Jefe Army. The Jama are still attacking from the North. They don't quit so easily and they hold a grudge for generations. This is how they fund their wars and weaponize against us. We can buy ibons from the yuvo to stop them. I've already discussed it with the council."

"So, you discuss with my council in my absence,"

Oba Kola paused. "And your brother, he should be there too."

"Sakin is barely here to know what happens in the capital. He spends all his time traveling or at the Sango Temple with Oju, studying something that'll do him no good later in life. You place so much of your admiration with him when I've been by your side since the beginning." Bode rose from the chair and walked to the window. "And you, baba. You aren't well to discuss any matters. Since mother's death you've been distant and your judgement is-"

"-Is what Bode?" Oba Kola's forehead furrowed.

"Questionable," Bode said dryly. "In fact," he faced his father, "the council and I think it's time for you to turn Jefe over to me."

"I knew that's what you really wanted to speak about. I'm not cold in my grave, yet you still plot to take over Jefe." Oba Kola shook his head. "The Gods don't grant wealth from selling our people, stripping them and their children from their homes and sending them some place strange." He leaned forward. "Wealth's in our land. It's in our food, our gold and gems."

Bode watched his father strain to reach his cup of tea. Oba Kola sighed after sipping from the cup before he asked, "Could you please pass me that jug over there?" He pointed next to Bode.

Bode stood motionless.

Oba Kola shifted his weight to swing his feet over the side of the bed. He reached for his walking stick. He shook his head at Bode's coldness as he boosted his stubborn body off the bed. "Where did I go wrong with you?" he questioned himself. He shuffled to the table in front of the window to pour a fresh cup of tea.

He grabbed his chest while he sipped. When he finished he walked over to the chair Sakin sat in before leaving. Weakly, he grabbed it and tried to pull it toward the table in the middle of the room.

"Can I get a little help? Please!" Oba Kola commanded more than asked.

"You have servants for that."

"But I'm asking you. I'm asking my son."

Bode growled at his obligation to his sickly father. He ripped the chair from his weak grasp causing Oba Kola to stumble a bit. He slammed the legs of the chair in front of the table. Oba Kola shuffled to the table. He sighed as he relaxed in the chair.

"Want to play me son?" Oba Kola started resetting the ayo board. "You'll lose like you always do," he chuckled at the thought since he rarely beat Bode in ayo.

Reluctantly, Bode sat down on the other side and reset his side of the board. Oba Kola made the first move. Small, glass stones clinked as they transferred from one hole to the next.

"If you want more money, work out a trade agreement to mine their land," Oba Kola suggested.

"Why agree when we can take the land and sell the people?" Bode sat back with his fingertips pressed together in front of his chest. "Baba, you're not thinking about this clearly."

"I'm thinking about what's fair and the balance of life. This moves people to join forces with you, knowing you respect them and their cultural systems."

"I'm not asking for what's fair. I'm asking for a king!" Bode gradually shouted. He regained his composure before he continued, "This isn't any different than us taking our enemies as slaves beneath our heels."

Oba Kola's eyes raised from the ayo board. "What've you turned into?"

"Oba!" Bode stood. His father's eyes climbed the sky.

Oba Kola calmly rose from his seat. "No my son. I AM OBA!" He slapped his right palm against his chest. "And you, you're a prince who has much to learn about ruling this kingdom. You'll fail Jefe and our Ancestors if you do so with greed and innocent blood."

"No baba. You've failed. A compassionate heart leads to death by the enemy." Bode shook his head. He walked to the table by the window. He watched the small, green leaves float in the jug after his thigh bumped the table.

"I wish your mother were here to talk sense into you. At least, when she was alive you tamed yourself to try to please her. You won't listen to me nor care what your brother thinks. Where's all this coming from son?"

Bode smirked at the question. He thought about the evening he sat with a small man who summoned an ancient demon to speak with him. "Just like you I have my own diviner."

"Oh." Oba Kola gazed quizzically. "Tell me son. What did your diviner say? There are many incompetent ones out there." Oba Kola walked steadily back to his bed to sit down.

Traveling many miles through burning sands and dense foliage, Bode searched for the darkest cave in the mountains. Stories told of a midnight dark being whose eyes flickered like yellow flames. It dwelled in the forbidden cave. This evil being granted requests almost instantaneously.

An accomplished feeling swept through Bode once he found the legendary forbidden cave. In the cavern, on a heap of bones, a man sat murmuring to himself as he ate the meat of a cadaver too old to recognize. So crazed, the man (thought to be human) didn't acknowledge Bode when he announced his presence. The man threw pieces of bone with meat still attached behind him. Bode stated his presence again. The man mumbled riddles until he called the being Bode wished to see.

When the being appeared, it was clear the man had no power over it. He cowered with fear in a dark corner. He was merely a slave, trapped to do the demon's bidding. The demon rose from black smoke and spoke with a deep, cringing voice. Each time the candle light hit the being, that part of it dissipated and returned when the light captured another side. Bode had never seen anything like it. He was sure this was the course of action to get what he wanted.

"It said that I'll be an invincible king. That no one could destroy me as long as I make a sacrifice." Bode turned around.

"What sacrifice is that?"

Bode walked over to his father's side and fixed the pillows as Oba Kola laid down. Bode picked up one more pillow and smiled. "Your life for your throne." Bode placed the pillow over his father's face. "And I won't stand by as you king your favorite son."

Both men struggled. One struggled for life in a coughing fit while the other struggled to contain his demented laughter. Oba Kola's hands drifted from Bode's wrists. He laid flat. Bode placed the pillow aside. He tipped the cup over on the nightstand and positioned his father as if he were reaching for it. When he found the room acceptable Bode walked towards the door. Before he left he looked over his shoulder. "I'll be sure to tell the council what you said."

Meta

Children played while their mothers and grandmother's chatted with a watchful eye. Their talk resembled old laughing guinea hens. Sakin leaned on a
tree trunk and admired Ade's beauty. While she drew
the mountainous view in the sand with a twig, the river
painted a portrait of her deep brown complexion and
high cheek bones. She hummed the song her mother
sang to her and her siblings as she smiled at the children running by.

Sakin loved Ade from the moment he became
interested in girls. She accompanied her father, Dele,
Oba Kola's chief merchant, on many occasions. They
played together and attended school. Their favorite
pastime, when she wasn't hanging out with his sisters,
was making fun of Bode as he trained seriously. Another was mocking the villagers' stone face haggling in
the marketplace or running through the market fright-

ening the animals and causing commotions with the merchants. Bode reprimanded Sakin for his childish endeavors. Sakin disregarded his brother because nothing was going to keep him away from the girl he loved. It was at this river he snuck out of the aafin with Ade to swim, something most young adults did. Here they shared their first kiss beneath the moonlight.

One of the boys recognized Sakin since he was known as the fun prince. "Omoba Sakin Adesine!" the boy shouted as he pointed. All the children and abled bodied dropped to their knees and placed their forehead to the ground. Ade bowed her head.

"Jowol dide," Sakin said. "Please, rise."

Many returned to their chores. The children ran up to play with him. He kissed the girls on the back of their hands. He told them how much he admired their smiles and dainty behaviors. "You'll make fine wives someday little ones," he said as he patted their hair. He rough housed the boys, wrestling a few to the ground. He stopped to let them all pounce on him and let them win by pinning his arms and legs.

Ade got up and dust specs of sand off her lapa. A little boy knelt down next to her and swiped her drawing with his hand. She grabbed her things and walked towards the market beyond the forest and over the hill. When Sakin noticed Ade leaving, he got up and gave each boy a cowrie.

"I must go. My girlfriend's leaving me."

The boys ran away laughing and teasing Sakin. The girls pouted as they walked back to their washing stones.

"Elęwa," Sakin called out to Ade.

"Yes, it is a beautiful day."

"I was talking about you." Sakin scanned the ground for flowers. He found a yellow one with many petals near her feet. A worker bee, finished extracting nectar, flew away as Sakin picked the flower and placed it behind Ade's ear.

"Careful Omoba Sakin. You wouldn't want your bride-to-be to cause you any problems."

"So you heard about that?"

"The aafin walls have many ears. It seems your

fleeting affairs are coming to an end."

"So, you've heard about that too?"

"You think I'm a deaf fool?"

"No, I think your brilliant. Far better than any other woman in the kingdom."

Sakin smiled, revisiting his first time amidst her soft shivering thighs, kissing her lips gently as they listened to the festivities within the aafin walls. They blossomed into adulthood together, each carrying a piece of their family's aspirations upon their shoulders. Before that moment of laying in her bosom, Sakin knew he wanted to marry Ade. Many times he wanted to ask his father to make the marriage arrangements, but petty wars within the kingdom's factions thwarted the conversations. When his time with Oju came to an end his father made him the oba's amiable voice. While serving his father, Sakin drifted into a world of name-less women bestowed as gifts that he somehow cleverly managed not to marry.

He waited. In his culture a man could be well into their twenties before taking their first wife. Then his mother died. A vortex ripped through his chest and crippled his father to the point of no recovery. Seeing his father live though such a loss made him push Ade away. Now his brother and the counsel decided what marriages would take place and Sakin and his sister were next.

"What business do you have at the market?" Sakin asked as they started to walk on the trail through the forest.

"I have to set up a meeting between the businessmen and my father. They want to talk about the high tributes."

"Oh, that's easy to resolve. Cut their tributes until the harvest season. Sales from crops will be better. They deserve a break from this rough season."

"I know. I've suggested that, but your brother is defiant as a mule. He keeps talking about funding wars."

"We're not fighting anyone. We've been peaceful since Bode won the North War. Sure there are minor disputes, but that's not unusual."

"Yeah, but Bode is always looking for a war or scrimmage. Oba Kola and the counsel advises against taking small villages that can barely defend themselves. Bode does it anyway. He keeps talking about expansion."

"You invite them into the kingdom. Set up contracts. They shouldn't be forced or you'll always have a mad mule."

"He's selling the people." Ade frowned.

"My father mentioned something like that to me. I told him I'd look into it, but I haven't found anything substantial."

When they made it out of the forest, Ade stopped at the top of the hill. Her glare followed the leaves and insects riding the breeze into the capital city. The market, not too far from the aafin, was busy. People walked the paved trails from their compounds to the market. Men walked along side their sons reining a mule pulling a cart full of goods. Some boys pulled cattle along. A steady stream of women walked gracefully to and from the river with jugs of water sitting on top of their head. Children ran from the forest back into town after playing and fetching fire wood. The city's opaque luster of red clay buildings with thatched roofs and housing arranged in gated compound clusters with animals grazing green grass never ceased to amaze her.

Ade love coming to the capital city. Her family resided in a village called Jembe, located further up the river. Her great-grandfather, the headsman of the village, accepted an agreement with Oba Kola's great-grandfather to join Jefe not only for protection, but for the trading opportunities. Jefe traded with other kingdoms and villages as far as the sea and the North with the Turegs, sometimes with the Jama when prices were fair and they were on peace terms, and with the Bariba in the East. Jefe's ships carried gems, gold, weapons, corn, spices, animals, artistry, money and more. Ade's great-grandfather saw an opportunity for his people and his family. He passed that trade contract down to his son. This eventually trickled to her father Dele who now trained her.

Throughout their long relationship, Dele and

Oba Kola became close friends. Oba Kola invited Dele and Ade to stay regularly as royal guests. In this way, Dele could access all financial activities to accomplish his job. Together they made Jefe one of the richest kingdoms. When Dele's wife (Ade's mother) died, Oba Kola's priests helped prepare the burial arrangements. He even gave Dele two woman to help take care of his first wife's obligations. Later, Oba Kola's wife died. They grew closer through conversations on how to deal with such a loss.

Knowing that being apart of the royal bloodline greatly enhanced his family's position, Dele offered his most prized daughter, Ade, to wed one of the princes. He found it difficult to marry Ade off because men shied away from an opinionated woman with a powerful position. Oba Kola accepted the offer since his admiration ran deep for the young beautiful woman. However, those plans were halted in wake of Oba Kola's growing illness. He let Bode and the counsel decide marital arrangements for his children that reached marriageable age.

Dele's relationship with Oba Kola afforded Ade many luxuries. Her favorite was traveling. She attended rites of passage banquets, weddings and harvest festivals all over the kingdom and beyond. She sometimes bumped into Oju who travelled with his students, Sakin being one of them at the time. Ade managed business well. She could quote anything and negotiate with anyone anywhere, often obtaining bargain contracts because she was appealing to the eye.

Sakin watched Ade take in the scenery. Each found something more as if they had a new set of eyes. She turned her head and realized he was studying her like he had when they first met.

She cleared her throat. "How's the oba?"

"His light's waning. It's as if he has nothing to live for any more since my mother's death."

"He has you. You should visit him more."

"I should visit you more." Sakin grabbed her hand.

Ade snatched her hand away. "We can't keep doing this?"

"What do you mean?" Sakin asked quizzically.

"I mean you're about to be married to a princess and I have to marry someone else because you waited too long."

"Someone else? Who?" Sakin stepped back.

"Ode Akata, third born of Essien Akata. He'll make a fine husband and business partner."

"You can't marry that man. I forbid it."

"You forbid it? What do you propose I do?"

"I propose you wait."

"I can't. It's my duty-"

"-Wait anyway."

"Until when. Until you're done spreading your seed in barren holes? Until you marry a princess and fall in love? I'll be old and gray waiting on you with no children of my own."

"Wait until I can take you for myself. It won't be long. I'll just marry this princess and marry you too."

"It's too late. It's happening two weeks from now."

"No, Ade. I can't lose you."

The ẹsos running up the hill startled Ade. They

were yelling for Sakin.

"Ade. I…" Sakin reached out for her.

The ẹso in front to the pack stopped and bowed his head before he spoke, "Oba is dead!"

Merin

After nine days, the king's burial arrangements were finalized. Oju travelled tirelessly to the aafin for the burial of his friend. He and Sakin prepared Oba Kola's body and performed sacrifices for an easy transition to the home of the Ancestors. Strangely to them, Bode declined his obligations to help.

Sakin stood princely as a line of people came to give their condolences. Bode stood tall and kingly. He grunted every time any one said, "Oba Kola was a fine king, the best of our time."

Oba Kola's wives cried with their children. They feared their fate under the new ruler. They watched him grow cold as he got closer to his throne day. Sakin tried to reassure them. He promised he'd make sure they were sustained. However, they knew their home would be moved as Bode expanded his own family. Worry filled them as they watched the various ceremonies unfold.

Vibrant dancers masqueraded through the streets, soulfully uttering melancholy praise poems days before the burial. Food and drinks were bellied by mourners throughout the kingdom. The people stayed festive to commemorate the king. Although revered, death was also celebrated since one was returning to their source away from the market of endless suffering.

Artisans donated sculptures and painting of the oba. Opportunist produced as many commemorations as they could to sell to visitors and residents. Sakin liked the paintings. They captured his father in his younger years when he was happy. Bode, on the other hand, shunned every donation. He told Sakin he didn't want to be reminded of their father. Anger settled with every step Sakin took through the halls when he found his brother erected painting of himself instead. Questioning Bode's odd behavior led to quarrels. Confounded, Sakin watched his father's essence be erased from the aafin.

Sakin longed to see his father again, to hold his hand and talk about life. Sakin missed the laughter that filled the halls, the touch that soothed his soul after his mother died, the victorious grin after a game of ayo.

He spent nights with his father's corpse rubbing his hand and kissing his forehead. He quietly pondered. If he stayed with his father in his final moments he might've adverted death. Health is more important than business. But, he wasn't there. Oju once told Sakin when they returned for Ife's funeral, "when it's time Iku takes who's His. We can't be sad about the natural cycle of life. Instead, we must celebrate the gift of life by enjoying memories of our loved ones."

Sakin sang when he felt himself slipping into darkness. His voice cracked between sorrow and joy. Sometimes he heard Ade humming on the other side of the curtained room. She waited for him as he prepared his father's body, a ritual Ade did for her mother and helped with Ayaba Ife.

Oba Kola's spirit would be done visiting people he knew after seven days. On the eighth day, Sakin and Oju bathed the body by candlelight with a herbal elixir. They delicately rubbed lavender on the stiff body. Oba Kola's wives tailored an outfit for their oba. A bright, red buba with gold embroidery and cowries sewn around the neck line, down the chest was his final outfit. The jewels embedded within the cowrie crown danced as light grazed upon them. White lilies laid around him. Oju folded the oba's hands atop each other on his belly. Sakin carried the floral scent in his mind.

His mother carried a different smell for her burial rites. She smelled like honey and amaryllises, the faint aroma returned whenever she crossed his mind.

On the ninth day, Oba Kola's body was ready to be laid to rest. Sakin assisted Oju as he sang odes of life and death, wishing Oba Kola well as he travelled the various realms back into total consciousness, becoming one with ALL. Oju puffed smoke over the body and watched the wind carry it to the heavens. Pallbearers carried the body through the capital city to the marketplace where villagers congregated to pay homage to the oba.

Iyalase, dressed in white, posed as a market woman selling palm oil, shea butter and honey. She watched the ceremony from within the crowd. No one saw her transformation from a large white bird with red and black striped feather tips. They barely recognized the old woman in their midst. The people who did acknowledge her presence walked by respectfully as they did all older women within their culture, careful not to offend the Íyami since one never knows when they choose to take human form to walk among them. If any one were to look directly at them they'd see

Iyalase's eyes were so bright they shined like stars in the heavens,. She watched the ceremony as she called out in her ancient voice, "Epo, ori, oyin…" repeatedly while music vibrated the earth.

Bata drums boomed and shekeres rattled as a masquerade spirit- Egungun, dressed in long panels of multi-colored cloth, swept the earth as it danced around Oba Kola. Its brisk winds fluttered the sheer white silk that canopied the corpse. Egungun carried a light-brown wooden staff with a wide open circle for the neck. Egungun waved the staff over Oba Kola's body while chanting a deep, inaudible phrase repeatedly. The people gasped, some screamed, at the sight of Oba Kola moving amongst the living. The most powerfully prepared medicines caused such an event. Up until this point, the animated dead was a fable told by very old storytellers who saw it before in their lifetime. With fear and reverence all the people prostrated. Bode's impatient indifference made him slow to follow.

The oba, still covered by his white veil, sluggishly danced with Egungun. Egungun led Oba Kola next to Sakin who grabbed his father's hand and kissed it. Next, Oba Kola danced in front of his wives and other children. Their tears created a river outlining his feet. Oba Kola grunted as Egungun led him back to his resting bed. His body laid down, quiet as before. Every one stood up.

When Egungun danced by Oju, he stood and danced. When the spirit danced by Sakin, he stood and danced. Egungun danced past Bode to two of his younger brothers, twins of the second wife. The twins stood and danced though unaware of what was truly going on. Oju motioned for the pallbearers to follow the dancing masquerade towards Oba Kola's resting place.

Bode stood to follow. He stopped when Egungun scurried back and forced him to his seat. Egungun crossed the staff across Bode's neck. He minutely bled. The spirit dared Bode to move. Bode decided against the idea as his eyes dug into the earth between his feet.

Egungun eerily said, "Today, we bury our son. Tomorrow, we come for your head." The deep groaning voice sounded like many behind the mask. The staff pointed again towards Bode. He stood and backed away slowly until he was far enough to turn and leave the ceremony with Tekun, his newly appointed ẹso. So busy dancing no one noticed the gesture.

Egungun swirled around and continued to dance. Sakin's heart lightened as the drums possessed his feet. He danced with the masquerade spirit towards his father. Before the twins could question the sensation, they were taken by the drums. Their bodies moved in ways it never did before: jumping, rolling and arms lightly colliding into each other in an improvised warrior dance. Oju succumbed to the rhythm pulsating through his body. He shuffled slowly like a man beyond his years.

Children watched with amazed eyes as Sakin and his brothers, dressed in red, were carried by the wind, suspended in air for unusual lengths of time. They returned to the earth on all fours like a panther. The children began to move with the beat of the cow skins, like their parents who were caught in a rhapsody, the moment feeling everlasting.

Drums mourned from great distances. Villages celebrated the oba's home-going from where they stood. Voices shuddered the leaves high above them, traveling high and far like golden eagles. Each city had its own verse in the long orchestrated ballad.

People followed the Adesine family. Birds circled above. Animals walked in procession (even those hidden by forestry) along with spirits unseen (unless with a keen eye). Everybody sang and walked towards Oba Kola's final resting place. When they arrived, the people kept singing outside as the family proceeded behind closed doors, laying the king in a plot at the base of the aafin next to the kings before him.

Seeing everything to the Ìyami's satisfaction, Iyalase transformed back into the white bird. She flew into the sky until becoming a beacon of light.

Marun

Small pockets of mourning festivals were held
throughout the kingdom. Men and woman, in their
respective circles, talked about Jefe under the rule of
the king-to-be, Bode. Business people shared concerns
about their businesses since Bode already used them to
finance his destructive plans. Mothers and wives feared
for their husbands and sons who'd definitely had to
enlist in Jefe's Army to fight insensible wars. The only
thing the citizens knew for sure was Bode lacked the
warmth of his parents and was as brute as a rhinoceros.
Aafin guests kept this in mind as they chatted softly in
Arèmo Bode's presence, making sure not to offend him
in any way.

Soft, fast-paced musical notes from marimbas,
koras, shekeres, bells and drums glided throughout the
banquet room. Bode sat on a throne in the large room
decorated brilliantly with blue silk table cloths and gold
vases holding bouquets of colorful blossoms. Broasted
boars sat on silver platters, along with the meats of

various fish, goats and cows. There were large bowls of boiled yams, beans and salads. Fruit freshly picked from the forest tempted the guests with hues of reds, blues and yellows while palm wine flowed in abundance.

Tekun stood near Bode who held his jaw while waving the other hand as presenters offered gifts hoping to gain favor.

Oju was disturbed by the insensitive Arèmo Bode and the absence of Omoba Sakin.

Ade stopped Oju as he walked by her. "Baba Oju, have you seen Sakin?"

Oju shook his head. "No dear, but when you find Sakin tell him we have more work to do in the morning before the sun rises."

"I will. You rest well," she said as she bowed her head.

"Adupe. You too."

As Ade searched the room she saw faces in wet palms and circles of people whispering. She went near the throne finding Sakin's seat empty just as before.

"Ago, Arèmo Bode," she said as she bowed her head. "Have you seen Sakin?"

Bode's eyes lit up as he shook his head and placed his back against the throne. "Sit." He pointed to the seat next to him. Ade loathly sat with her back straight and her head held high. "I think it's time you and I had a talk about the future of Jefe."

"Trade is going well Arèmo Bode. Our scouts are finding more caverns to dig for gemstones. They want to go across the river to the mountains though. Our hills have only a fraction…"

"No, Ade. Jefe needs a queen like you."

Shock almost veiled Ade's face, but she quickly erased the feeling to put on her negotiation face. "I'm sure your council has many other prospects in mind. I hear the king in the East has many beautiful daughters ripe for marriage. The alliance may prove fruitful."

"No princess is as beautiful as you nor proficient in work. You know Jefe almost better than me. This union would be the best." He grabbed her hand. "Besides, I've already aligned with the Jama by securing a princess for Sakin."

Resisting the urge to take her hand back, she let him squeeze it uncomfortably. "I'm flattered," she lied. "But we should speak about this after your coronation. All marriages have been put on hold until a proper mourning period is over."

Bode grunted, pretending to understand. He knew she loved Sakin yet her decline to be the queen stung. He bedded many women as spoils of war or concubines, but he only wanted Ade if for no other reason than to take her from his brother who always seemed to have everything, even the crown in people's minds. "Everything happens when I say it happens," Bode replied.

"May I be excused? My baba looks like he needs to be tended to." She rose as Bode released her hand. "Arèmo Bode." She bowed before she turned to leave.

She grabbed a cup of wine from a server's tray, swallowing it in one mouthful. She placed the cup on a table before wrapping her arms around her father's arm turning him away from Bode. "Baba."

"What was that about?" Dele asked as he looked slightly over his shoulder.

"Have you spoken with Arèmo Bode?" she asked as she continued to walk her father to the garden.

"Bẹẹni." Dele nodded with an eager smile.

"So you knew Bode was going to propose," she asked once they were in the garden.

"We talked briefly about it after Oba Kola passed. I've already told Essien. You said yes right?" Both joy and fear resonated on his face.

"I said he should have more appealing prospects."

"And he let you get away with that?" He shook his head. "Well, I won't. I've been too relaxed with you and your obligations as a woman. Your mother still criticizes me when she visits my dreams you know. This is a great opportunity for our family. You'll learn to love later. You will marry Arèmo Bode. You'll get no better offer."

"Baba!" She glare at him.

"No! You have to stop waiting on Sakin. Oba

Kola got too sick before he approved," he shook his head. "You'll do what he says or it'll be the death of us all."

Ade relinquished Dele's arm and stormed away. Music followed her down the hall and up the stairs as she went to a large sitting room where she sat with remorse and anger.

Bode watched Ade's dispute with her father and chuckled. He saw the moon halfway into the sky as he motioned Tekun to come near. Tekun bent over Bode's shoulder, placing his ear in a safe receptive area. "It's time," Bode said.

Tekun nodded. Three more ẹso replaced him as he walked through the side room where the council met past the corridor and into a field where soldiers waited beneath the moon.

Sakin leaned against his wardrobe as he looked at the moon. It peeked from behind gray clouds like a child playing hide and seek. The stars played too as constellations of former kings emerged from behind the clouds. His father was not there yet. He still had realms to go through before a configured landing place was present in the sky. He smiled at the thought of the reunion of his parents, his mother aiding his father on his passage.

He was sipping wine when he heard a knock on the door. For a moment, he ignored it wishing to be alone. He wasn't in the mood for a concubine to help his mind escape. The knock persisted. He answered it.

When he opened the door Ade was standing there, face fluffed by tears and a slight smile hoping for an invitation.

"Eléwa." He grabbed her shoulders and pulled her into his chest.

"I wanted to check on you. I wanted to make sure you're alright," she said as she fought the tears in her voice.

"Wa." He lead her by clasped hands to a sitting area.

"Bawo ni?" she asked. "How are you?"

"I'm ok," he said as he rubbed her hair. "I have better spirits when you're around though."

"I just wanted to make sure I'm around to help you like you helped me when my mother died."

"You've been helpful. You remind me life isn't all bad when I see you."

She grabbed his hand and kissed his palm. He placed his palm on her cheek. After a moment of eye gazing she broke it, interlocking her fingers with his in her lap. She took the drink resting on his knee and finished it before she placed the cup on the table.

She kissed his forehead then leaned back and placed his head on her bosom. She rubbed his hair as she hummed. The melody released the iron gates of his heart as he let the words slip from his tongue. "I miss him."

"I know," she said softly.

He felt uplifted when she finished humming. Music from the banquet room climbed the walls, but they focused on the insects, forest animals and birds stringing a symphony that floated through the window. He faced her.

"I have something to tell you." Her eyes roamed

the features of his face.

"Shhh." His thumb grazed her lips. He cupped her chin bringing her lips to his, watching as she closed her eyes to sink deeper into the blissful kiss.

Ade breath suspended in the moment. She always wanted more of him since the day she realized she loved him more than a brother.

Sakin knew now how foolish he'd been all those years, paralyzed by the fear of losing another person he loved. They gazed into each other's eyes, wordlessly painting a future. He was ready.

He leaned into her ear. "Mo nife o," he whispered. Ade freed one wrist and pushed his chest up until they were looking at each other. She needed to see him say it, to look into his eyes and know he was being truthful. Sakin understood as he always understood her.

"I love you," he emphasized. "And I'll never let you go. I promise."

His breathe was shaky as he rubbed her hair. His lips lightly touching hers. He laid next to her. She listened to his heart beating fast as she twirled his chest hairs. He kissed her forehead then lifted her eyes to his.

"You will be my wife." He grazed her cheekbones before he kissed her again.

Ade rested her head, but not her mind. She waited so long. Now it was too late.

"I have something to tell you, Sakin." She sat up to face him. "Your brother has asked me to be his wife. He and my father already agreed to it." Tears weld up in her almond eyes.

Sakin laughed at the thought.

"This amuses you?" Ade jerked her head a bit.

"Elęwa, Bode nor Ode will marry you. Bode cannot take what's not his." He kissed her forehead before resting it back on his chest.

"That's just it," she said, "I'm afraid he will."

~

Downstairs, gazing at Bode within the crowded room was Amadi. The young man hung around many of his uncles and men in the marketplace where he heard talks of how Bode would ruin Jefe. Discussions of his murder lacked fervor, but they were taken to heart by Amadi.

Amadi's father didn't take a liking to him since he was birthed by his least favorite wife. He wouldn't be given any title in the family and although handsome would receive less favorable bride options. Amadi decided- if he killed the man everybody loathed, he'd become a hero. Now was the perfect time since his father was away confirming one of his daughter's marriage proposal.

Amadi inched his way towards Bode's stage. He walked by the debauched gatherers unnoticed. Even Bode barely noticed him until he saw a flint of light moving off a long blade.

"Long live Oba Kola!" Amadi disrupted the noisy chatter as he lunged towards Bode. The three ęso were slow to react, only catching Amadi after the blade pieced Bode's chest. Red soaked his royal garb.

Bode grabbed Amadi's chest and maintained a stone face as he extracted the dagger. He threw Amadi down. The ęso beat Amadi with assegais until Bode halted them.

"Má sẹ gbe!" Bode shouted. "Stop!" Two ẹso held Amadi up in front of the king-to-be. "I have a far better punishment for the young man who dares to kill the king of Jefe."

The bound Amadi spat at Bode's feet. Bode punched him in the nose. Blood splattered. "Whatever punishment you have is better than living under your rule!" Amadi said as blood threatened to choke him.

"Find his family and take them all. Every single member of his bloodline. Have them march with Tekun." More ẹso came to carry out the orders.

Quietness filled the room. Everyone was too frightened to move. No one ever witnessed an attempted assassination. Some wished Amadi had succeeded. Medicine men tried to tend to Bode's wound. He waved them off and asked for more palm wine.

Bode's anger grew once he noticed how quiet the room remained. "Musicians continue. Everyone dance. Rejoice. Your king is not dead."

The party resumed as dismal collected people's

spirits. Their king was dead and if this was an omen, Jefe might soon follow.

Interlude

Dawn peeked through smoky clouds above crackling fire. In a small village outside Jefe's jurisdiction, the inhabitants slept. They were alarmed when Bode's soldiers set their roofs afire smoking them out of their homes.

The beaten Amadi and his large family witnessed the confused, defenseless people stumble into their courtyards. Their necks were snared by flying ropes, snatching them to the ground. Amadi, a young fool, cringed at the horror before him and his family.

Men were beaten or stabbed before they could grab their weapons. Young men tried to fight by their father's side but were overpowered. Women screamed while running after their children. Some children found hiding spaces mapped out for such occasions. Eventually, the children were found. Others, leery of their surroundings, tried to smother the fire with gourds of water. Their attempts were interrupted.

Tekun wanted to finish overtaking the village

before the sun rose. He accomplished that. The villagers watched their homes burn to the ground and their valuables thrown onto horses' backs. Men cursed as some of their daughters and wives were raped before them. They helplessly tried to get free. When they squirmed too much, they met the blunt blow of a club. The soldiers, whose sexual urges were replaced by the taste of blood, stabbed and bludgeoned the village elders. Babies were either tossed aside for furry predators to feast or cast into burning homes.

Tekun ordered his men to line the whimpering women and angry men up. They joined Amadi and his family with ropes around their necks connecting them to the person in front and behind. Their hands were bound behind their backs.

Once everything was finished all the people marched westward. The sun beat their backs. Village boys damned themselves for falling asleep near their drums on the outskirts of the village. They were captured before they could alert the village or call for help. No one expected this to happen when the oba was freshly buried. Many were still celebrating his transition into the stars.

It didn't matter. All was lost.

They marched- going further west than they could imagine. They reached a body of water that dwarfed their lakes and rivers. Like the others, Amadi lips were white and splitting from their extreme dryness. Their feet were swollen from endless miles of travel. Their eyes squinted as they emerged from the forest shadows to face the cool, glistening blue ocean that casted a salty perfume miles before they saw her. The yellow sun hovered as the water foamed at the banks of the beige sand. Their marching slowed as their feet sank into the sand. The sand scorched their cut, blistered soles.

A club against Amadi's back forced him out of the magnificent scene. He noticed ships along the coast and many people caged along the beach. The crashing waves ruminated the background as Amadi listened to his brethren's anguish. Amadi's cousin, a boy too young for his rites of passage, rubbed Amadi's back with his shoulder. Amadi turned as best he could towards him.

"When are we going back home?" the boy asked. Tears filled his eyes as Amadi's late response crushed his hope. "I want to go home."

Amadi couldn't find comforting words. He just stared from the corner of his eye at the little boy his actions cursed. "I… I'm sorry."

Amadi turned away from the weeping boy when he saw Tekun walk past the line of captives that snaked up the beach. He watched Tekun talk to a yuvo.

Tekun followed his instructions. He sold the captives for ibons and strong liquor then returned back to the capital city with Jefe's army.

A few days later, after seeing new weeping faces, the villagers were sent across the ocean on a gruesome trip to a strange land, wishing they had drums to thunder for help.

Mefa

Despite the council's suggestion of a longer mourning period for Oba Kola, the king coronation was set. A little past the sun's peak Bode was scheduled to parade around the city before settling in front of his courtyard. Baskets of gifts and chattel were prepared by the citizens to wish their new oba well. Elders instructed their families on proper behavior during such a ceremony. The council planned everything while Oju and Sakin took care of the spiritual work.

Oju sat confused at his divining mat as Sakin helped slaughter the sixth bull. The Gods still were not pleased. Oju's opele danced in the air before he released his grasp allowing it to fall on the mat. He threw his hands up in respect and frustration. After a few more throws, he softly swiped the configuration and placed the opele in a small gourd of water. There was nothing more he could do to please the Deities about this coronation. Sakin saw this and wondered how to make his brother an acceptable heir.

Before his death, Oba Kola expressed his wishes for an heir someone like himself and Ife to continue ruling. Sakin felt his brother could learn. At least, Sakin wanted him to because he didn't care about ruling a kingdom. He felt the empire would expand, even westward beyond the shore to a distant land he'd heard about, without his help. After the coronation, Sakin planned to go as far away as he could with Ade. They'd start a family, become yam farmers and palm oil merchants. They'd sit around their compound watching their children blossom. They'd change their names to live a bureaucratic free life.

Ruling meant he was responsible for thousands of lives, a responsibility usually reserved for the first born. Briefly, Oba Kola talked about breaking that tradition to make Sakin his successor.

"What about Bode?" Sakin asked Oba Kola as they played ayo the morning of his father's death.

"He'll do as I say whether he likes it or not. I chose what's best for Jefe." Oba Kola grumbled.

"But baba, I have no experience."

"No one has any experience other that watching their father. It's not something you train to do. It's something you're born to do. It's something you learn as you go. Why do you think I made you my emissary? You understand people. He only knows war and I'm to blame for that. I will not have Jefe ruled by the monster I've created. I will not have nonthreatening people slaughtered and sold into slavery." He paused until his coughing fit subsided.

"But you don't know if that's what Bode's really doing."

"I know my son."

Sakin sat back and looked out the window. "I promise I will not let our people be sold into the enemy's hands, wherever they may be. I promise to do what's best for the kingdom."

Sakin thought about his promise as he rode a horse in front of the parade behind a wall of soldiers paving a way through the affable crowd throwing flowers at their feet. Bode was carried by six shirtless men, shielded from the sun by a sheer red canopied cloth with Tekun and other ẹso riding next to him.

Bode held his chin in one hand and waved at the crowd with the other. Pervasive boredom moved him to eat an apple and toss its remnants at a specta-

tors head. Finding it amusing, he had done it twice. The
first time he hit a small child who looked in every di-
rection to see who threw it. The second time, he aimed
for a man bending over to pick up something. The man
was hit on his way up. He argued with a confused man
nearby thinking he had struck him. The argument led
to a small fist fight another man broke up. Bode let out
a boisterous laugh rocking his traveling seat.

A stage was set up outside the courtyard adja-
cent to the entrance. Bode, Sakin, the council members
and the Iya Oba sat on the stage before a sea of citizens. More ęso wrapped around the stage like a skirt,
protecting the new head of the kingdom. Many of the
citizens were afraid of what their new ruler brought.
They envisioned war and gloom. Whether they saw
peace, tyranny or selfish gains, they stood awaiting the
Iya Oba to crown the new oba of Jefe.

Arèmo Bode dressed in red and gold clothing
wrapped around his midriff. A sheet of red draped over
his right shoulder covering his wound. Necklaces of
hyena teeth, lion claws, cowries and glass beads decorated his chest. His ankles and wrists were adorn with
gold bracelets. On his left upper arm he wore an amulet

he received from the dark spirit he visited again before the ceremony.

Ting… Bode remembered the sound ringing throughout the cave. A silver trinket fell to the ground at Bode's feet. He picked it up, its leather straps fell through his fingers.

"Wear this around your upper left arm and nothing shall wound you again." The black cloud wavered like smoke rising out of a pipe. "It'll make you immortal like the Gods you silly humans praise." The eery voice laughed through the hauntingly dress cave. "But, as you know I need something in return."

"What will you have me do?" Bode asked as he strapped the amulet in place while the spirit laughed.

Bode smiled as the time neared. Opening speeches and prayers were made by the elders of the council. A red bird perched on the log roof of the stage, patterned like boxes to let sunlight touch the platform. It was Iyalase.

Iya Oba, the matriarch entitled to crown the king, walked her plump figure over to the woman holding the crown on a plush, purple pillow. The tall crown, decorated with tiny glass beads, depicted blue birds on a yellow background sectioned off by white columns. Atop the round crown was a bird with outstretched wings. When Iya Oba's chubby hands held the crown, long strands of deep blue beads hung. She walked over to place the crown on Bode's head.

Bode, kneeling on one knee, looked at Iya Oba's face. Behind her, he saw the red bird diving for the crown. Its belly rubbed against the top of the outstretched figure almost tipping it out of Iya Oba's hands. Iya Oba recovered graciously. Never had she witnessed or heard of such an occasion. Her eyebrows furrowed as she thought of what to do. Doom flooded her soul. If the Great Mothers revealed their true feelings about Bode, she couldn't continue without repercussions.

Her old feet shuffled back towards the woman holding the pillow. She placed the crown on it and sat down. Whispers breezed through the crowd. An Iya Oba openly rejected the new king. An expression unknown even back ten generations.

Bode rose from his knee and faced the crowd. The muscles in his jaw tightened. His mind searched for words to say. Open aversion hadn't swayed Bode

since his mother slapped him on a busy day in the marketplace in front of, what seemed in a child's mind, the
entire kingdom. A baby goat cried out while he rubbed
his new blade across its stomach painting its white fur
with droplets of blood. A tear excited more pain on his
scolded face. Ife's delicate trembling hand was about
the only thing he remembered about his mother. It was
the only thing he saw as he heard his mother call his
actions "monstrous."

The monster spoke. "The late great Oba Kola
wanted to see Jefe prosper. He wanted to see our culture spread throughout the region so that all civiliza-
tion celebrate our wonder. My father wanted me and
my brother Omoba Sakin to lead you and your families
into a golden future. I accept this task," he said as he
walked towards the crown. "And as you all know from
my previous conquests, I never fail. We never fail. As
I wear this crown all of Jefe wears it with me because
we're all the children of the mighty leopard. This isn't
just a crown. This is Jefe!" He placed the crown on his
head. Its long blue strands, veiling his face, hung until
they reached his knees. Ceremonial drumming com-
menced.

Everyone knew the Iya Oba had to crown the king. It's been done since the beginning of time. However, no one would challenge Bode. So, instead of incurring his wrath, they cheered the new king, Oba Bode.

'Look at me now mother. My monstrous acts grew this kingdom you call home. Now, I'm its king. Not your precious Sakin. Nothing's going to stop this journey. Not even a wretched foul.' Oba Bode thought as he walked off the stage into the courtyard and into the aafin. The doors slammed behind him.

All of the council members looked at each other. Every fear they had spoke through their eyes. Agreeing with the now Oba Bode up until this point, without his father present, left them two decisions. They could either continue to follow him risking dishonor among the Ancestors or death with honor. Essien, a chief, decided he'd succumb to neither as long as he could. He replaced the dismal look his peers wore with a smile as he celebrated the new oba.

Ade turned to Sakin as she clapped, confusion riddled her face. "You know what this means right?" Sakin nodded. "We can't leave," she said. Sakin shook his head. "You have to become oba."

Sakin stared at the crowd. Their grinning faces masked their true feelings. Many woman wiped tears away as they held their sons closer while looking at their husbands who stood stern as they clapped. He saw huge clouds swarming the aafin with thunderbolts walking beneath like legs of a bee. Highlighted in yellow was an elderly man and child dressed in rags with dirty sunken faces and ribcages telling a story of food deprivation. Flying black skeletal spirits hauntingly laughed as they ripped the old man away from the frightened child's arms.

"A king fights for and protects his people. Upholds their cultural and spiritual systems. If he does anything other than that, which many have and many will, he goes against the king of us all Sango. Our traditions are what makes us who we are. It's how we sustain ourselves. Without them we're nothing." Oba Kola sat comfortably in his bed. "You will be king, Sakin."

Sakin released Ade's hand as he stood up. "Bẹẹni. I have to."

Meje

Oba Bode reached a festive feeling when he arrived at the coronation celebration. He passed the line of people bearing gifts to the throne and sat down. Tekun stood on Bode's right side staring into the distance. Sakin sat in a smaller chair left of Oba Bode.

A nice young bare breast servant took gifts after they were presented to the king with well wishes and placed it on a red clothed table. There was livestock, jewelry, golden forged vases with rubies and vegetation. The poorer people gave whatever they could spare. After the gifts were handed to the servant the presenters bowed. Some of the people brought gifts for Sakin as well. Sakin held their gifts while they attempted to bow, stopping many before they made it to the ground. Oba Bode grunted at the sight.

"Ma se gbe!" Oba Bode said as he stood. "Enough. Let us eat." He walked over to the table and listened to men as they spoke of gold, money, trade routes and weapons.

Sakin joined Ade standing in the corner by a banquet table. She grabbed a vine of grapes. She plucked a purple orb and fed it to Sakin. They both smiled as they gleefully grabbed at each other, glancing around every other second to see if anyone spied their unorderly behavior. Adunni, Sakin's younger sister from Oba Kola's second wife, spied them and walked up to them happily.

"Well look at you two." Adunni said as she grabbed a piece of fruit from a serving tray. "Still inseparable after all these years of barely seeing each other." They all chuckled. "Did you see what happened? That old woman not crowning Bode because of silly little bird. I know Bode has his faults but…" She trailed off as she looked into their uninterested faces. "Anyway. Have you heard?" Adunni leaned in closer.

"Heard what?" Ade asked.

"I'm going to marry a prince. A Jama prince. I know that's disgusting, but they've agreed on our marriage on peaceful terms." Adunni smiled showing her beautiful teeth. "I hear I'll be the queen."

"Maybe Oba Bode changed his mind," Ade said to Sakin.

"No. You know Bode never changes his mind. This'll be the second time he's done it. They must be getting impatient," Sakin said.

"Who cares what those beasts think? When I become queen they'll all bow to Jefe." Adunni looked at their unconvinced faces. "Don't you understand? We've finally won." Adunni stopped Essien as he walked by. "Olori Essien."

"Omoba Sakin. Binrin Adunni. Ade." Essien bowed.

"Olori Essien's escorting me to my wedding. Isn't that right? He set it all up." Adunni pridefully smiled.

Essien smiled. "Bẹẹni. I am. We leave in a week."

"What does the council say about this? Marrying my sister off to the Jama. How is she safe and their threats stop?" Sakin asked.

Essien looked at Adunni then back at Sakin.

"The council advises against it. But, the oba gets what the oba wants." Essien bowed before he excused himself. He studied Ade and Sakin suspiciously. He motioned for Sakin to lean in closer with his index finger. "I urge you to remember your place," he whispered while he looked at Ade. " The oba gets what the oba wants," he repeated. He slightly bowed his head and walked away.

"It'll be alright Sakin. The council advised father against a lot of things and look at Jefe now. They don't know everything." Adunni tried to hide her disappointment. "Excuse me." She walked to the banquet table and grabbed more fruit to eat. Ode greeted her at the table. They both laughed with the mirth of children.

Ade rubbed Sakin's shoulder. "I'm sure she'll be fine. Maybe the Jama have changed and really want peace," she said unconvinced.

"Maybe. But, Bode hasn't."

Sakin stared into Ade's eyes then smiled. Tekun alerted Oba Bode of their interaction. His forehead furrowed at the sight. Oba Bode excused himself to tend to the situation.

"Thief!" Oba Bode heard an ẹso yell as an elderly man was wrestled to the ground. A ball of pounded yam rolled out of his hands towards the feet of a little girl, her light brown skin smeared with smudges of dirt.

"Baba!" she shouted as two ẹso picked him up underneath his arms and carried him away. The young girl ran after them. A woman stopped her.

The guards threw the fragile old man at Oba Bode's feet.

"Oba this man's a thief!" an ẹso said.

Chatter simmered as eyes peered at the disruption. Rhythm slowly died as musicians looked to see why movement stopped. Within the crowd Sakin kissed Ade's hand before he walked towards his brother to help calm the event.

"Please, Oba. I was going to live with my son, but I found the village in ruins. My granddaughter is the only survivor. We seek refuge in my home city and tell you about the atrocities we've witnessed, praying our new king provides justice. I'm too old to work and we're hungry," the man explained as he graveled at the oba's feet. "Please, spare me," he begged.

Oba Bode clenched his teeth, disgusted by the man's fragility. He stared at him while he watched his guests within his peripheral.

"There's no room for thieves behind the capital's walls. Especially not one at my gathering." He pulled Tekun's machete from his hip and swung the blade over the man who now looked up. He brought the blade down.

Sakin emerged from the crowd catching his brother's arm. The crowd gasped. Their eyes widened. Essien walked through the crowd until he was in front, confident in Omoba Sakin's ability to quell the situation that was about to break taboos.

"Please, Bode!" Sakin pleaded. "Let a court decide such matter."

"I am the court!" Oba Bode shouted at his brother.

"Then please judge fairly," Sakin whispered.

"This man and girl are just hungry. We have more than enough to spare." He waved at the abundant display of food. "You can even let him run small errands for the council and I to pay for his food."

"Are you questioning the Oba?"

"No," Sakin sighed. "I'm reasoning with my brother. Let this man go and be the oba mother prayed you'd be. The great one our people needs."

Oba Bode lowered the machete to his side. Fire still lingered in his eyes. "Go. Before I change my mind."

The old man rose with Sakin and Essien's help. He hurriedly stammered away towards his grand-daughter with outstretched arms.

Oba Bode turned to Tekun and nodded. Tekun lifted his spear and threw it at the man's back. The tip exited his chest, stopping near the girl's face. The girl gawked. Ade ran and grabbed the girl pressing her head into her chest as she carried her away into the aafin.

"I changed my mind," Oba Bode chuckled.

"Brother." Sakin grabbed Oba Bode's forearm.

"Oba!" Bode corrected Sakin, snatching his arm away. "And this is my crown to wear." He walked away. "As you were," he shouted before he sat on his throne.

Everyone forced themselves to return to their conversations and festive behaviors. After retrieving his spear Tekun ordered the ẹso to throw the man's body into a field for scavenger animals.

Sakin walked past his brother into the aafin with a tight jaw glaring at his brother. He went to his father's room to think. He punched the red clay walls until his anger stopped boiling. He leaned back in the chair he sat in during the long days of conversation with his father. He thought about the Jefe Kingdom under his brother's reign. He reflected back on their childhood, Bode's quick to anger temperament and detachment.

Sakin understood people, yet he couldn't comprehend the darkness inside of his brother. He watched other the children in town. They were affectionate towards each other. His brother abused him, making Sakin grow thicker skin to fend for himself.

When Sakin was sent to the temple to study with Oju, he learned to stay calm by watching Oju. Oju stayed even tempered as people cried about their lives. Relationships were broken, sometimes forbidden by rival families. Children disappeared never to return. Businessmen lost everything turning their family into beggars. Women lost babies, a malevolent spirit preying on their wombs each time. Oju told him, "through it all one must remain calm and steadfast." Sakin understood and often felt their pain because he watched his aunts, cousins and father's wives go through many of the same things Oju saw on the mat. However, the one nurtured in the same environment as him he understood the least. His other brothers and sisters were jovial without a care in the world. However, Bode had this ever brewing anger inside of him.

Ade entered the room after knocking on the door.

"A servant said I'd find you here." She closed the door behind her.

"How's the girl?" Sakin asked.

"Her name is Tocarra. She's not good. She has lost everything." Ade walked behind Sakin. He grabbed her hand as it rested on his shoulder. "She and her grandfather came from a village that was destroyed. Her mother told her to climb into a tree to hide. She says her father was murdered while trying to defend their burning home. Her mother tried to help her father, but was pushed and hit her head on a stone. Her older brother was one of the first bound during the attack and was marched westward. After the attackers left she mourned her parents while everything smoldered around her. Her grandfather brought her back to the city to tell the king and stay with some friends until he could figure out what to do next."

Sakin frowned. His temples bulged as he listened. "Does Tocarra have any idea who did it?"

"She said the same man who murdered her grandfather was in her village the night of the attack." She walked around to face Sakin. "Your brother ordered the attack."

They heard a knock on the door. "Oba is looking

for you miss." A male servant said with his eyes focused on the floor.

Ade looked at Sakin quizzically.

"Go. I'll wait for you in my room." Sakin whispered before he kissed her.

Sakin ruminated on his brother's disgraceful actions. When he left his father's room he found Essien waiting in a study room with his legs crossed and his hands folded on his knee.

"Omoba Sakin. May I have a moment of your time?" Essien's deep voice said as he rose. His tall, thin body looked like a budding boy's body. Essien came from one of the most wealthiest, if not the most, bloodlines in Jefe. Essien was a chief that travelled back and forth from the capital city to his village eastward. He had five wives in both locations with over thirty children and a whole compound of aunts, uncles, brothers and sisters including a dozen his father's widows as wives that he took care of. His compounds were so large they looked like small villages.

"Olori Essien. Forgive my manners earlier. How's

the Akata Clan?" Sakin asked.

"My family is well. Please forgive my manners. I've been busy as you know negotiating various marriages," he paused. "Your father was a fair king. Jefe lost one of their greatest."

"Adupe. What is it you want to discuss?"

Essien smiled. "Why... Jefe of course."

Mejo

Ade entered Oba Bode's meeting room. Her eyes adjusted to the low lighting. Candles on the table outlined Oba Bode's face. As she got near the table, he covered up a map with a tray.

"You wanted to see me, Oba Bode?" She stopped at the table.

"The girl. Give her to me," he demanded.

"Is it true?"

Oba Bode smiled, his straight, pearl white teeth were illuminated by the flames. "What difference does it make?" he asked.

"Oba, those people were defenseless people mourning the death of your father."

"Bęęni. They will make good slaves for the yuvo."

"How are you any different than the Jama?" Ade asked.

"I'm not."

Tekun entered the room followed by two ęso.

"Everything's in place. There are men digging the earth now. It's positive for minerals. No gold though."

Oba Bode sighed. "The yuvo asked for gold."

"They accepted the trade for now. We're storing the ibons."

"Da." Oba Bode drank from his golden cup.

"We've could've asked those people. They could've been apart of Jefe," Ade said.

"They would've hated us and did nothing we asked." Oba Bode stood up. "Leave us," he commanded Ade. "And Ade I will have that girl."

"Let me keep her as my servant," Ade pleaded.

Oba Bode looked her over then nodded. If he were to have a successful marriage with her a few concessions would have to be made. Satisfied, Ade turned to leave. "Shut the door," he said when she got closer to the threshold. She did as he commanded, but hid on the other side.

"Is there anything else?" she heard Tekun ask.

"Bęęni." Oba Bode waited until he felt Ade was

a safe distance away. "Kill the Iya Oba. Make it look like an accident. An omen for not crowning me. And Sakin," he paused. "I need you to take some men to go after him. The people are too fond of him." He rubbed his beard.

"You want us to bring him to you? Tekun asked.

"No." Oba Bode sat down. "Take the ibons. We'll see if we got our monies worth. The people need to see they have no other option for a king."

Ade smothered her gasp with her palm. She backed into a servant who dropped a tray of fruit. She ran to warn Sakin. Her breath escaped once she reached his room. When she arrived she knocked.

"Wa!" Sakin watched Ade appear from behind the door. "Elęwa!" His feet carried him half the distance for a hug. "What's wrong?" he asked once Ade's outstretched arm stopped him.

Ade's voice trembled as she began to speak. Hearing the fear in her voice, he stroked her back. Sakin cupped her chin with his palm. "Oba is sending Tekun to kill you," she muttered.

Sakin's clenched his teeth and his lips tightened. His palm dropped from her face. He turned to walk to his wardrobe and opened it to weapons of his choice.

Ade's eyes widened at the sight of his weapons. "No!" She rushed to his back. "You can't or you'll give him what he wants, a dead brother."

"He has terrorized the people of Jefe and dishonored my father's name. I can't let him continue." He turned to face her. She could see the fire rise in his eyes and his muscles tighten as he turned to grab a double headed ax.

"You'll be dead before you reach him!" Ade shouted. "No. You must leave. Your the kingdom's only hope," she said as she reached for the ax.

"No! I must fight." Sakin moved forward.

"You have nothing but a double headed ax to fight the army of a treacherous king." She back towards the door to guard and listen for time.

"I have two axes." Sakin walked back to the wardrobe to grab another.

"That's not the point!" She rubbed her forehead.

"If you go out there to fight you'll die this hour. Your father and your father's father and all the honorable kings who built this kingdom will have died in vein. But, if you survive," she lowered her voice, "to come up with a better plan, come back with an army, you'll fight and you will win."

Sakin's shoulders lowered with desponded thoughts. He found reason in her words and hope in her eyes. He cast the axes back into the wardrobe and grabbed a long, black cloak. "I'll send for you when I'm ready. I'll have an army that defeats him. In the meantime, trust Essien," he said as he moved to cup her chin. He brought her lips to his.

They heard movement. "You must go now." Ade cut the engagement short.

Sakin stare at her deep brown eyes. He studied the curves of her cheek bones while rubbing her chin and lips with his thumb. He didn't want to forget in case he was never able to return. The back of his curled fingers brushed her cheeks before he covered his head with with the hood of the cloak.

He opened the door looking both ways down the hall. "Leave this room. If they catch you, they'll kill you." Sakin told Ade before he ran down the hall.

Riddled with fear, Ade forced herself to move behind the door. She exited the room closing the door lightly. She rushed down the hall. She heard footsteps marching. She prayed she wouldn't meet them. She stepped to the side to hide in a small, faintly lit room.

Tekun stomped towards Sakin's room with a small army of men. His face was fixed with furrowed eyebrows and a clenched jaw. Tekun thought Sakin was amiable, but he had no quandary about murdering him or any one else. The oba's orders were his orders, whether viscous or not. His only existence was to satisfy the king.

Tekun flung the door open. His temples bulged when he found the room empty.

"You men search the entire aafin. You search the perimeter," he commanded.

Two ęso stepped into the room to search for clues while the commanded men went off to their respective missions. Others followed Tekun as he stepped out to walk down the hall.

Sakin waited on the side of the aafin for an ideal moment to pass unnoticed. He ran by a man with a mule pulling a cart full of goods. He walked alongside the cart looking around every so often. When he looked ahead, he saw boys kicking a spherical bundle of leaves tied by twine. One of the boys noticed Sakin. He and the other boys ran towards him. They grabbed Sakin's cloak, pulling it off in an act of trying to pull him to the ground. Sakin tried to get them to stop. They thought he was trying to fool them like he had done in the past.

"Ma se gbe!" An eso noticed Sakin trying to get away from the boys. "Stop!" The eso ran towards them.

"Are you warriors?" Sakin asked the boys as he dropped a bag of cowries for them.

"Of course." They all responded with a fist beating off their chest.

"Then run interference," he said as he ran away. "Beat that man and his friends up."

The boys created a miniature wall in front of the ęso chasing Sakin. One boy threw sand in an ęso's eyes. Another took a guard's machete and spanked him. One ęso was tripped. When he fell to the ground, the boys pounced on top of him. Unaware of what he grabbed, a boy held the ęso's long, black barrel rifle and pointed it to the sky. His little finger curiously pulled back on the trigger releasing an explosion that knocked him down. The boys scattered in various directions and the people nearby dropped to the ground in confusion. The ęso picked up the weapon, poured powder down the barrel before he ran back to his mission with his disoriented peers following him.

Sakin looked back when he heard the gun fire. Darkness veiled the sky as Sakin ran for the forest over the hill where it would be easier to hide. The guards followed him into the forest. Sakin heard more explosions behind him. He screamed out in pain as he grabbed his shoulder. He looked at the blood run down his arm and through the cracks of his hand. He rested by a bush to examine his wound. Heavy breaths waved the leaves near his face as he thought about an escape plan. His rest was cut short when he heard voices and footsteps near him. Sakin bolted for the river.

"This way." He heard one ęso yell. More explosions followed.

Bullets pierced leaves. Birds flew out of their nests into the moonlit sky. When Sakin reached the riverbank he jumped in. Bullets dived into the water. Sakin was hit again in his upper back. His breathing was interrupted. Water covered his head. The ęso reached the shore and fired at him again this time hitting his leg. He struggled to reach the surface. The river current held him under and carried him away. The ęsos fired one more time. They were satisfied when they saw blood run with the river.

~

In a panic, Ade looked for her father. She found him talking with Oju in the large hall. They were looking into the front courtyard, talking about the strange sound they heard.

"Baba Oju." Ade ran to him then bowed her

head. "Oba has sent guards after Sakin with ibons."

"What?" Oju and her father questioned with a bit of disbelief.

She stopped speaking when she saw Tekun enter the courtyard followed by ęsos. She turned when she heard footsteps behind her.

"Oba," Tekun said as he walked pass Ade to Oba Bode.

"Is it done?" Oba Bode asked.

"Bęęni. But, just to be sure I have guards searching down the riverbank. He was shot several times. There's no way he could swim to the other side of the river."

"What?" Ade started to walk behind Tekun. Her father held her back.

"This is senseless," Oju exclaimed.

"Shut up!" Oba Bode shouted at them. "If there's no body he may still be alive." He turned his attention back to Tekun.

"Oba, I doubt it. Even if he's alive there's no way he could survive the waterfall further down the river.

He'll surely drown. Or be eaten."

Oba Bode agreed. He walked past Tekun to Ade. "Now that my brother's gone you don't have him to hold you back. You will be my queen in the next three days and bear my heir by the end of the next harvest," he smirked.

Ade spat in his face. He wiped away her saliva as he laughed. Before his hand could make it across his face, he slapped her to the ground.

"Oba!" her father yelled out as he went to her aid.

"If he can't put you in your place, I will," Oba Bode said as he walked away.

"I will not marry you," Ade said as she held her burning face. "I will not marry an abami."

Oba Bode stopped. He nodded for the ęsos to siege her father. Dele tried to wrestle out of their grasp. They kicked the back of his knees forcing him to kneel. Oba Bode untied his machete. He held it in his hand as he knelt in front of the plump aging man.

"You've done yourself a disservice. I'll try to

clean it up by marrying a woman that no man wants. She doesn't cook or clean. She just runs her mouth with opinions, ideas about love and counts money. Do you know what our marriage would mean for your family? For your people?"

"Bẹẹni, Oba." Dele briskly nodded.

Oba Bode nodded with him. "But, she doesn't." He reached for Dele's hand. Dele grabbed it. "Let us teach her." Oba Bode helped Dele up. "If you don't give me your hand, I'll take his." He brought his machete down over the Dele's wrists lacerating his hand.

Her father screamed out in pain as he held his wrist in fruitless, painful attempts to stop the bleeding.

"Baba!" Ade ran to his side and tried to help him by removing her gele and tying it around his wound.

"You will marry me and you will bear my children." Oba Bode threw the hand down at her knees. "If not your father will suffer the same fate as my brother." He watched her lips part but stopped her before she spoke. "And your homeland, Jembe, is it?" he asked as he rubbed his beard, savoring the fear in her eyes at the sound of her village's name. "It doesn't matter. The yuvo can use them in the new land too." He walked towards Tekun. "I see the ibons work fine. Get an army of men ready to head to Jembe."

"Wait," Ade said as she rose. Oba Bode turned to her. "It'll be an honor to be your wife." Ade bowed her head.

"Bẹẹni," he smiled. Oba Bode walked over to Ade and grabbed her by the waist. He brought her face to his and kissed her, prying her lips open with his tongue. "Bẹẹni." He released a hearty laugh.

Mesan

Laughter saturated the river currents. Sakin opened his eyes to find the source. The laughter was flirty like an alluring woman blended with the innocence of a child.

Schools of colorful fish swam past him. Some nibbled on his body in search of a delicacy. The water was crystal clear. He could see the men after him like he was standing in front of them. They didn't seem to see him. He relaxed into the current avoiding a test of their sight.

He watched blood float over his shoulders. His pain subsided even as he lifted his leg to touch the leaking hole. The object's entrance was not as jagged as an arrowhead nor thin like a throwing blade. It was small and rotund. It was an unusual wound.

"Sakin." He heard a woman's voice call followed by laughter. He looked around, but saw no one.

Sakin felt he was a safe distance away from the ẹsos to surface. Tall, deep green algae trapped one of his legs as he tried to swim up. He tried to free his legs. His shoulder refused to carry out the assignment, his body in fear of pain.

"Sakin." He looked around again. He forced his good arm to unwrap his foot. He jolted up when a beautiful woman with a deep brown complexion face with smiling eyes brightened by the moon appeared. Slowly a body appeared before him; neck, shoulders, melon breasts with brown erect nipples, voluptuous torso decorated with dainty brass coins that dangled with the sway of her hips. She reached her arms up, exposing wrists full of brass bracelets caroling as they touched each other.

"Sakin. Gbogbo epere. Everything's better." Her hands rested delicately on his cheeks before she kissed his lips.

Sakin wasn't breathing anymore. When he entered her world the need ceased.

"Wa." She grabbed his hand as she turned to

swim away. Below her hips were bright, yellow-orang-
ish scales that led to a wide fin. So amazed at the sight
of the fin transforming into smooth legs, Sakin didn't
realize when they was within her space.

They were still suspended in water, but they
moved with the ease of being on land. She laid him in
a bed on his side facing a mirrored wall. The brightness
of the colors created light within the room. He watched
her hips as she walked towards a table with a large,
brass, oval mirror sitting on top. She grabbed a yellow
lapa with orange blossoms and wrapped her waist. She
sat on a stool in front of the mirror dabbing perfume
on her neck. When she placed the small amber bottle
back, she grabbed a bronze clip that was sculpted as a
bird with a long wing span. Its claws were designed to
pin her hair that tightly curled as it dried. She smiled at
him as she pinned her hair, her breasts rising with her
arms. The mirror reflected a mural.

She got up and walked to a tall, brown vase.
With the curl of her fingers water streamed out of the
vase and covered her hand. She walked over to Sakin

and knelt beside him. When her hand touched his shoulder he shuddered at the coolness. She began to sing as she massaged his back with the water that stuck to him like honey.

It was the same melody Ade hummed the night of his father's burial. When they was alone he always heard her hum it. She said it reminded her of her mother.

Osun mo me o o.

Olomodi mo me o.

Ololodi mo me o.

Mo pe o sowo.

Mo pe o somo.

Mo pe o si aiku.

Mo pe o si oro.

Eniti nwa omo ko fun lomo.

Emi ko fe odi,

Emi ko fe aro.

Omo daradara ni ki fun won.

Sakin felt sleepy as he watched her place slippery water moss over his wounds. She continued to sing, her

voice as soothing as a bird. He closed his eyes, dream-
ing he was in Ade's arms, oba of Jefe.

Mewa

"Tani se?" a man asked when he found Sakin-breathing. The man dressed in a white buba and had a long beard that covered his neck. His beard stiffly hit his chest as he spoke. "Who are you?" he asked again.

Sakin's eyes ached when he tried to open them to see his surroundings. "Elęwa. Obinrin. Omi," he said as he turned to his side to push himself up. He failed.

"What woman in the water?" Tose motioned for his men to search along the bank for a woman. "You're alone." The man looked at the water himself. "Tani se?" he asked again when he looked at Sakin.

"Osun," Sakin said weakly before he passed out.

Osun. Tose thought about the river Goddess as he sat next to Sakin. Years before all the wars and his losses, a beautiful woman, who smelled like the world's most beautiful fragrance, came to Tose in a dream. She told him he would find a man by the river who'd save

Owura and promote him to an even bigger status than village olori. He didn't understand as he sat next to her on a ledge behind a waterfall. At the time, his town Owura was peaceful, lucrative and his elders just appointed him chief.

"How would I know?" Tose asked as he watched the woman walk towards the ledge.

Laughter bounced off the cavity's walls as she turned to face him. "You just will." She laughed as she transformed into the mist and rain of the waterfall.

Later, Tose met a traveling diviner who gave him the same message without knowing Tose's dream. By then he prayed for the man as he lost son after son in battles with nearby villages, desperate not to be overtaken.

Tose's men wanted to leave the stranger arguing he could be a murder, rapist, thief or all. Curiosity filled their leader who thought this must be the man. Watching his exasperated soldiers bind the stranger with vines Tose whispered to himself, "It has to be you."

Iyalase, in the form of a white bird, perched on a

branch above watching from the time Osun laid Sakin on the riverbank until he was bound. She travelled tree to tree as he made his journey with the men.

The vine tied around Sakin's wrists chaffed his skin. His feet explored the new terrain for days. The path, layered with fallen branches and jagged rocks, pierced his soles. His crusty mouth begged for droplets of water.

Sakin forced his weak limbs to keep moving forward, straining like he was waist deep in mud, limping because of his injured leg. When he tried to stop or was too weak to walk, the horse he followed dragged him.

None of his captors expected him to survive the journey. Incoherent, Sakin didn't even realize they took him captive. The men didn't understand why their commander wanted to know more about this strange man with bullet holes stuffed with water moss. They thought he was dead when he fell from the heavenly waterfall until they saw him crawling out of the river then collapsing on the beach.

Sakin was tied to a tree near Tose's area while

the men set up camp. Before Tose retired he gave Sakin something to drink, a piece of game and a mat. Sakin ate ferociously and rested in pain.

Days later Sakin heard welcoming drums. He feared he was in Jefe since the welcoming call was similar. His heart beat fast as he tried to pull against the weight of the horse led by Tose. His resistance waned as an unfamiliar city shielded by a wall of logs appeared.

Across the field, women and children ran to embrace the men. Shrieking cries of those who loss their beloved rang in Sakin's ears. Tose continued into the village, down the paved roads to a large compound filled with animals and small playing children. A woman in a light blue dress with a matching head wrap stood in the courtyard. Tose handed the reins to the woman.

"Clean this man up," Tose said, "and tell my eldest son to fetch Baba Fasola." Tose walked to his four wives who hugged him one at a time before they walked into one of the biggest houses of the compound.

The woman took Sakin to a small abode where a stack of hay waited for the horse outside. Her eyes suspiciously looked over Sakin and his wounds as she untied him from the horse.

Sakin followed her inside the hut where she sat him on a mat. She poured some water in a cauldron and started a fire. Across the room was a shelf where she grabbed some cloths and a fresh sheet for him to wrap himself.

"You try to leave they'll find you and they'll be more successful than the people before at killing you," she said over her shoulder as she placed the items on the table.

"What village is this?" Sakin asked.

"Owura."

Sakin had never been to this village during his travels. He hadn't even heard of it. The people spoke with a different dialect, but the words meant the same as far as he could tell.

"Tani okunrin?" he asked. "Who is this man?"

She turned around and looked pass him out the

window. "He's my father-in-law. His name's Tose Balogun. The general of Owura's army. The chief of Owura."

Sakin noticed the admiration in her voice slighted with pain.

She looked at him seeing the real question in his eyes. "Whether he's a good man or not depends on you."

Sakin nodded.

She went to check the water. When it was hot enough she used a piece of her dress to grab the cauldron's handle and poured water into a wide calabash. The steam rose as the water splashed against the vessel's walls. She opened a dark bottle and poured a few drops into the water.

After placing the cauldron back over the fire she poured in more water. She waited a bit before she checked the heat by waving her wrist over the cauldron. When it was just right she put a bowl of okra and corn inside and sprinkled it with salt and pepper.

She grabbed the cloths on the table along with the calabash and walked over to Sakin. She knelt before him. From her waist she grabbed a small knife to cut the vines. Each shift of the blade made Sakin grimace. His wrists moistened with fresh blood. The stubborn vines were slightly congealed because his wrists tried to heal. Sakin heard the vines unsticking as the woman's small hands unwrapped them. She placed the vines and knife at her side then soaked some cloths in the water before she gingerly dabbed his wrists.

"What's your name?" Sakin asked to distract his mind.

"Morayo."

"Where's your husband Morayo?"

"Dead."

Sakin thought about how close he was to death. The Goddess in the river saved him and he was forever indebted to her.

Morayo looked into Sakin's eyes when his silence lingered.   "And who are you?" she asked.

Sakin thought about his old life. He was no longer the prince of Jefe. He was slave now who barely escaped with his life. He missed Ade and Oju. He prayed they'd be spared from his brother's wrath.

Oju explained to him in one of his earlier conversations. There would be a time when he would no longer be the prince but a man in his own right chosen by the Deities and not just lineage. That he'd become despised. "In that time, you have to decide for yourself who you truly are-" he could hear Oju say, "since we are all trying to discover for ourselves."

He looked back into her light brown eyes long and hard as if he was trying to convince himself. "I am Sakin."

Mokanla

The ẹso didn't find any trace of Sakin along the river. Even though his body wasn't discovered he was presumed dead. Those who loved Sakin mourned in private. A funeral wasn't planned since Oba Bode announced his brother was a traitor to Jefe. The people pretended to believe it in Oba Bode's face in fear of being called a traitor next.

Adunni was sullen yet excited to get away from the clutch of her eldest brother who was never satisfied with anything. She imagined life could be better with the Jama, even though the citizens of Jefe considered them savages since they were always engaged in a war they called Jihad. At least, that's what she was breed to think about her father's enemy.

Adunni arrived at her traveling seat, a square bed draped by long, purple curtains that would sit upon the shoulders of four men as she travelled north with Essien.

"I'm sorry for your loss," Essien said as Adunni stood looking at the aafin.

"There is no loss. Sakin was a traitor," Adunni said sadly.

"Right." Essien nodded as held out his hand to help Adunni onto the bed.

Adunni watched the capital of Jefe grow smaller as they travelled into the forest. She knew she'd never see Jefe again. They travelled all day. Every once and a while Adunni lifted up the curtains to watch the trees of the land she called home and to get some fresh air.

She sat uncomfortably. Before she left, she had to be given a medicine to help her bleed on her wedding night. She had to prove to her husband he was the only man she had ever been with which she cursed herself for now. She could feel the ants moving inside her, crawling and biting her walls. She was instructed to remove the ants the day after she left. She would slightly heal to where there would be no more bleeding until her wedding night. The intercourse would aggravate the wounds to make her look pure.

When they reached the burning sands of the desert she was given a change of clothes. A long, indigo dress with a flat head wrap covered everything but her face. She had to dress like this for the rest of her life.

"Let us talk about your family-to-be Adunni," Essien said as he sat down beside her in front of a camp fire.

Adunni looked at him interested enough although her mind was on Essien's son. They had a long goodbye before she went to the woman for her medicine. She didn't fault Ode for not asking for her hand in marriage. In Jefe, you had to be given a princess, not ask for one. Princesses were gifts or strategic pieces to bind royal bloodlines. She loved Ode, but she loved the luxury she was afforded as a princess more. Her position was powerful if her father were still alive. If anything were to go wrong, she could've gone back home to her father and beg for justice. Now with her brother being oba her tears would fall on deaf ears. So, she prayed her husband would love and accept her even though they were enemies forced to hold peace. At least, that's what she prayed until Essien kept talking.

"You will wed the Emir's son Saddiq Umar. Emir Umar set up this arrangement with your brother in order to insure peace. Truth is your brother wishes you to be a spy. Oba Bode doesn't want peace. He wants to cripple his enemy." Essien watched Adunni's rotund eyes widen.

Oba Bode told Essien he would reveal Adunni's obligations to her. However, his interactions with the yuvo, his marriage arrangements and declaring his brother a traitor distracted him. Essien advised against the plan. If it were Omoba Sakin marrying the Emir's daughter they could draw the Jama in to celebrate then ambush them on their way home, crippling them by taking their king. Instead, Oba Bode wanted to hinge ending the generational war on a weak little princess and kill the brother that gave Jefe hope just by breathing.

"You're dressed like this because the Emir is converting to Islam," Essien continued. "He's throwing the Deities his Ancestors worshipped away for a foreign god called Allah. Are you aware of the religion?" He watched Adunni nod. "They pray several times a day which I think is backwards since they engage in Jihad. The religion took hold like wildfire up North. Oba Kola refused to convert. That's why they call us enemies. I pray your Ancestors protect you because after I hand you over I cannot." Essien grabbed her hand and squeezed it. "You delicate flower. Your father would've never sent you to fight a man's war. Yet, here you are."

"Any advice, Olori Essien?" Adunni half smiled.

"Bẹẹni. Become Saddiq's poison. He's a likable young man similar to Ode." Essien could see Adunni's heart stop for a moment at the sound of his son's name. "Try to get along. Then perhaps you can persuade him little by little in Jefe's favor. He will be the next Emir."

"And if I can't?"

"Then you'll die. Mentally, spiritually or physically before or after you've killed one of them." Essien left her by the fire to retire.

Adunni held her tears back and her head high.

"Everything will be alright," she whispered to herself. "If this were a perfect world."

The hot sun of the burning sands dried them out. Adunni transferred to a horse to let the men carrying her rest by dragging her seat. When they reached the city's sand walls, Adunni understood why they called them the sand people. The high walls were unimpressive. However, inside, Adunni's eyes gazed at all the colorful garb and textile work lining the street leading to the palace. The palace stood taller than the aafin with more radiant colors that glimmered when the sun touched it. Next to the palace was a modest sized building Essien told her was the mosque where they prayed. Although smaller, it outshined the palace.

Emir Umar, his son Saddiq and his ministers waited at the top of the tall staircase for Essien and Adunni. Adunni was so hot she wanted to take off her clothes. She was afraid she sweated off all her essential oils. Essien instructed her to cover everything but her eyes. Their hosts floated out of the ground as they reached the top of the stairs. Adunni bowed before the

Emir.

"Emir Umar. Oba Bode sends his sister as he promised. He apologizes for not attending the wedding since he tends to his own at this time. He sends me in his place," Essien said.

Emir Umar called for a slave to come forth. "Set our guests up. We feast before sunset," he said before he turned to leave.

Adunni was impressed with Saddiq. He stood tall and blacker than anything she had ever seen. His dark brown eyes and thick eyebrows looked into hers beneath his head wrap that covered his neck and chin. His pinkish lip slightly smiled revealing dimples. Adunni felt relieved. She was given a fine looking husband that she already felt safe with. His father Emir Umar on the other hand intimidated her. He stood tall with a round belly under all his indigo and brown clothing. He had a thick white beard that looked like it pushed his mouth in and a mean face.

Emir Umar laughed more with Essien during the feast. Adunni dressed in a blue kaftan which she was careful to cover herself underneath with a skirt. She wore a head wrap that she was able to remove enough to eat the delicate beef served to her with groundnut soup, a dish her palette enjoyed the most.

After dinner Adunni was allowed to walk around the palace. She ventured to every wall letting her fingers brush the blue and yellow tiles as she walked. A group of women stood on the veranda, overlooking the entire city and beyond the wall, giggled like she and her sisters used to do before life became complicated. She approached them. The women looked at each other as if confused by her tongue. Adunni was taught to speak several languages and their dialects. It was apart of the curriculum for people of importance in respective kingdoms, so she knew they understood her. They walked away laughing.

Adunni stayed to watch the moon rise over the homes that spawned out of the ground.

"It's beautiful right?" Adunni heard a deep male's voice behind her. She learned it was Saddiq when she turned around. She quickly turned away to cover her face with her scarf and lower her eyes to the ground. "It's alright Adunni. I know this is a new world for you. Besides, I can't wait tomorrow to etch your beauty in my mind so my dreams are as sweet as the moon tonight."

Adunni eyes rose from the ground onto him as he stepped next to her. "You're kind."

"Do not mind my sisters. They are simple minded and don't take to outsiders well. I on the other hand do." Saddiq looked over the veranda.

"Princess Adunni," Essien startled her a bit. "I believe its time for you to retire. You want to be well rested for your wedding day," Essien said when she turned around.

"Bẹẹni." She bowed after she excused herself. Essien bowed to Saddiq and followed.

On her wedding day everyone greeted her with well wishes of a successful marriage and many children. The Emir's ministers talked to Essien about the peaceful union between the two kingdoms. Adunni dressed colorfully in orange and indigo to match her husband's attire. She was flattered by Saddiq's flirtation and warmth of the nearness of his body. He stayed hand and hand with her adverting his father's glare. Her mother-in-law kissed Adunni and hugged her every chance she got.

"I am so sorry your brother could not attend the wedding," her mother-in-law said as she walked locked in arms with Adunni. "You're more beautiful than I imagined. But usually, pretty girls don't come untainted." Adunni kept her lips shut with a smile. "I would've preferred a nice moslem princess but I guess deliverance is open for all. I will teach you so my grandchildren can have a proper life."

Adunni hid her agitation with a nod. "With your help I will."

The night went long with string instruments strumming light high-tempo melodies. The people danced and drank while they told old stories that each other knew. The ceremony of bridal negotiations and vows took place gleefully. Adunni was even surprised and appreciated his sister-in-laws taking her to a women's only room to get henna tattoos painted on her hands and feet. Saddiq traced the henna patterns all evening tickling her.

Adunni felt a hand on her shoulder after she reached the food table. She was glad she enjoyed the food because her hunger grew every day. She tried to hid her appetite by eating small portions, but she was never satisfied until she reached her room where she ate privately what her servant girl served her.

The hand belonged to Essien. "Have you enjoyed yourself?" he asked.

Adunni nodded. "Everything's nice. My mother-in-law is a bit much, but they usually are. Right?" Adunni joked.

"I'm glad," Essien smiled. "It's time. I'll escort you to meet your husband for your wedding night. I'll be heading back to Jefe tonight."

Adunni nodded. Gloom filled her eyes. She wasn't ready to be on her own. She never had to be. Crying was not an option. Praying was something she rarely did, but now with each step she prayed to her Ancestors for strength and protection. To her that was Essien staying or taking her back home until she reached the door with her husband waiting on the other side. Then she prayed her secret wouldn't be discovered. Otherwise death would come sooner.

Essien knocked on the door. While he waited for the crack he hugged Adunni and kissed her forehead.

"If this were a perfect world you'd be home married to a respectable Jefe man. But it's not. We live in a world full of evil. My last word of advice; fight until your last breath." The door cracked. A slave came out to receive her.

Essien watched as Adunni was pulled into the room and the door shut behind her. She was stripped bare and led to a tub filled with warm milky water. She relaxed in the water. She bathed. A cold hand on her shoulder startled her.

"Don't be afraid. It's me," Saddiq said. He chuckled at her alarmed reaction. "Do you know why I had this waiting for you?" He watched the hump of the back of her head move side to side. "It's because Jefe women are known to be some of the most unclean."

Adunni rose out of the tub with water splashing out of the it as she turned around to face him. "Is that how Jama men talk to their wives? The one they vowed to protect?" she angrily asked.

"No," he bluntly said. "This is how we treat slaves." Saddiq threw some light brown clothes at her that was thinner and less coarse than burlap. Adunni protected her face from the impact with her forearms. She almost slipped in the tub. "You are not my wife. I married my wife a week before you arrived."

"My brother, the oba of Jefe, will kill you for this." Adunni stepped out of the tub to cover herself with a lapa from her things sprawled over the bed. If she collected them fast enough she could reach Essien before he left. She prayed it was him on the other side of the door when she heard a knock. When she turned around she saw several large men enter the room. Horror filled her eyes when she look at their sharp weapons.

"Your brother didn't even have the decency to

fulfill the deal in person. He's a weak leader. I'll take over the Jefe and become Emir to the North and South. All who don't convert to the true religion will be sold or killed." He looked at Adunni's refusal to give into fear and chuckled. "Starting with you."

Saddiq turned around. "Take her," he commanded his guards before he turned to leave, closing the door to her screams behind him.

Mejila

The days Tose spent hidden away with his wives balanced him. That time took away the seeping remnants of anger left behind from the war. He harmed his enemy enough to keep them away for now, but he lost more. He tried to place all the images in the back of his mind as he walked to Morayo's hut a few days later to check on Sakin who, hopefully, was the token to end his troubles. He kissed Morayo on the forehead and asked her to go to the market with his wives to shop for a new outfit for the village mourning taking place for Owura's fallen warriors the next day.

Sakin slept on the mat near the wall. Tose read a book while he waited for Sakin to wake.

"The man who hunts glory finds death. But, the man who finds sweetness in life is loved and has glory," Tose read as he heard Sakin shuffling to sit up. He lowered the book and continued. "I was told to help a man in need. I was also told to engage in war with a nearby village. He closed the green book and sat it down on the floor next to him. "I lost my son in that war."

Tose reminded Sakin of Oju when he first arrived at the temple, speaking in riddles while maintaining a calm air.

"I don't know why I continue to listen to the oracle," Tose chuckled as he shook his head. "It's cost me my sons and left me with a lot of grief."

Tose continued to study Sakin. He poured a cup of water and handed it to him. "Tell me. Do you know what loss is?" he asked as Sakin grabbed the cup.

"Bẹẹni." Sakin nodded before he sipped the cool water.

"Where are you from?"

"I'm from Ibeju, where the Sango Temple resides."

Tose faintly remembered the village. He rarely got new visitors. The ones he did get were trying to invade his land for its fertileness and resources. He spent most of his life defending the home of his Ancestors.

"Why are you running?" Tose asked.

"My brother has conspired against me."

"Those holes?" Tose pointed.

"Caused by ibons. Healed by the Goddess Osun."

"You've healed miraculously." Tose looked at the leaf bandage slipping off Sakin's leg. It revealed a wound free of infection and nearly sealed by new skin. Tose extended his hand to help Sakin stand up. "Walk with me."

They walked slowly around the compound at first. They rested by the gate of the compound and waited for Morayo and his wives' return.

Tose and Sakin then walked around the village. Tose talked about the many wars that plagued Owura since his youth. With each war he lost a son. Most of his daughter-in-laws returned to their families in their homeland to save their sons. Tose never argued with their reasoning. Morayo was the only one who stayed with her young daughter Kisi, Tose's favorite grandchild.

Tose explained how the wars were initiated when

gold was found in their earth. He cursed the precious mineral. Minerals were just objects not people. The villagers wouldn't even mine for them. Living was more worthy of their short time on earth, especially since loved ones were lost every other season either from illness or war.

Sakin agreed that life was worth more than gold. He suggested the people move elsewhere.

"Anywhere you go there's wealth in the ground. 20 years from now visitors will find something else they like and try to take it," Tose responded.

Sakin saw that truth within his brother's actions. Every year, Bode told their father of some new thing worth a fortune to foreign traders. When the market for that thing plummeted he searched for other resources. After finding wealth in a new mineral, Bode would raid the village killing most of the people out of savage fun.

When Sakin and Tose returned to the compound, they sat around a fire and continued their conversations. It was like the long nights Sakin spent with his father laced with Oju riddles. Tose's wives tended to their husband and this stranger who now became a guest. By dawn Sakin and Tose became friends. They felt as if they were kindred spirits.

Sakin accepted Tose's invitation to seek refuge in his compound. He was sure his brother wouldn't find him, especially since he didn't really know where Owura was located or how far the river carried him. Tose allowed him to stay in one of his son's hut. At least one of his four wives made sure he ate. Eventually, it became Morayo and her daughter tending to Sakin's needs.

Sakin loved smelling the meals Morayo cooked. It was more enjoyable watching and helping her prepare them than having the food brought by a servant. She taught him about herbs and spices. She compared cooking to the balancing act of life. After they ate, he'd play games with Kisi and told her stories of a prince and his adventures in a far away land. Kisi admired the prince's girlfriend, but she fell in love with the prince.

Metala

At the end of the harvest, Oba Bode and Ade had a beautiful wedding that Ade forced herself through. She was nauseous the day before. As she was crowned ayaba of Jefe, she vowed to her citizens she would protect them. Clamorous cheers and claps penetrated the city as she shared a distasteful kiss with the oba.

Their first night together they fought. Ade was too weak to fend Oba Bode off for too long. He found her battle exciting. He was used to taking things he wanted. Ade wouldn't be any different. When she grew tired she laid there as she watched the moon outside the window.

Sakin was gone. She only lived to protect her home village, the kingdom she now stood queen over and hoped to raise a heir to rebalance it. If that took too long, she was prepared to take the oba's life. She tried several times. Oba Bode found it to be a game. He wouldn't eat anything she brought him to eat and over-powered her whenever she threatened his life with a weapon. He wanted her even more. He wanted to break her spirit like a wild animal.

Oba Bode was happy and continued to be kind to everyone around him for days. When Ade confirmed her pregnancy, he was even happier- most of the time.

Oba Bode ripped through the surrounding villages, took people from their homes and sold them into slavery for profits. The citizens felt the lost spirits haunting the Jefe. Relocating was an unappealing idea since there wasn't any place to hide from the merciless oba. So, they stayed while he dressed his new wife and his subjects in the finest jewelry and attire.

Oju warned Oba Bode of his heinous acts. Oba Bode didn't want to hear about the repercussions of his savagery. He wanted to hear the citizens praising him for boosting the economy.

"Do you know what the yuvo actually do to

those people, our people?"

"Yes, I do." Oba Bode leaned back on his stool and smiled.

"Well, that's nothing to praise, no matter how you try to reason." Oju rose from his stool, placing his bag over his shoulder. "I can't continue to stand by a monster. I'll return only after the birth of the child. Ade deserves to know the child's future."

"That's if your welcome!" Oba Bode shouted. "I'd be careful if I were you. Ibeju might be next on my list."

"And I'd be careful if I were you. Sango will punish your acts severely."

"Did your opele tell you that?" Oba Bode eyebrows raised, imitating interest as he leaned forward.

"I don't need to cast for something so obvious." Oju turned to walk out the door.

Ade waited patiently for Oju who softened at the sight of her. His touch on her big, round belly interrupted her hand from rubbing it. His eyes met hers and smiled.

"I wish I could take you with me," Oju said.

"What's going to happen to Jefe?" Concern plagued her voice.

"The kingdom will remain broken until the chid reaches the age of seven. Then you will see a new era," he whispered as ęsos walked pass them.

"What will happen then? The oba seems to grow stronger every day. Towns become haunted whenever he steps outside these walls."

Oju grabbed her hand. "When the baby is born send for me. New information will be revealed then."

"You know something." Ade tilted her head and eyed Oju suspiciously.

"I always know something." He smiled as he dropped her hand softly and walked away.

Essien bowed as he passed Oju. His languid figure stopped before Ade. His lean body bent at his hips as he said, "Ayaba Ade."

"Olori Essien. I pray the counsel has been fairing well despite the oba's actions." Ade folded her hands on top of her belly.

"We've seen better times." Essien smiled. "Forgive me for not keeping up with you. I was away on family business. I had to bury a dear uncle of mine."

"I'm sorry for your loss. May the Ancestors accept him when he reaches the other side."

"Adupe. We should have a seat to catch up. I'm sure your feet are sore. My wives complained about that many times," Essien almost whispered as two ęso marched by them. He guided her to a nearby bench overlooking a floral garden of red and yellow hues. When they sat down he continued. "Please excuse my speech, my queen. I have a story that you may enjoy."

Ade nodded for him to continue.

"When I was a boy that dear uncle of mines had a wife that was promised to him. She was a young girl who deeply loved another. The man she loved was a traveling musician who planted the seed of dissent within her. My uncle was a very cruel man in his younger years. When he found out about the seed of dissent he snuffed it like a young flame. Afterwards, he buried his wife next to her lover," Essien paused and looked at the flowers outside the window. "If I were to give her a word of advice, I'd say flee before my dear uncle found out."

"I admire your story. Your advice however is misguided. Fleeing is not an option."

"Then another way should be found. I think I know an aunt who could help her should the time ever come. All the young woman should do is ask." Essien rose. "Ayaba Ade," he said as he bowed. "Just remember the aafin's walls has many ears…" Essien whispered as he watched a servant named Mofeyisade walked by holding a jug of palm wine about to enter the room Oba Bode used as an office. "… and more mouths."

Merinla

Ade screamed as she pushed. She squatted over a small prepared space within her room. Her servant held her arms and shoulders as she strained. One servant placed a cool towel on the nape of her neck.

Oba Bode paced outside the room. Tekun stood near him.

"Everything will be alright." Tekun tried to calm Oba Bode.

"It's too soon," Oba Bode grunted. "We got into an argument yesterday and I shoved her into the wall."

Tekun stood without blinking. "Everything will be fine," he replied.

"It's my first born. He better be fine." Oba Bode shifted his gaze back to the door muffling the shrieks of his wife.

"Oba. I have to something to discuss with you," Tekun said.

"Bẹẹni." Bode sat at the table next to the door. He lifted his cup for the servant to pour more wine.

"The yuvo are getting impatient with us. They said we haven't been fulfilling our quota and if we continue to fail they'll start raiding the towns in our kingdom."

"I give them thousands of men, women and children and they still treat me like this? What if we give them more gems?"

"As I'm sure your wife has told you, there has been an incident that killed over thirty men. It happened during the storm with high winds. Some of the tunnels caved in. Our workers are afraid to go back to the site."

"So, we have other mines."

"The same thing happened at those places as well."

"Well, make them. They can't sit around forever. Start cutting off their children's fingers. They'll return to work."

"We've tried that before. They are more afraid of

the gods than you."

Oba Bode threw his cup at the wall near Tekun's head. The startled servant dropped the jug of wine on the floor, shattering it. Tekun remained unmoved.

"You stupid girl. Clean this up now!" Bode shouted.

"Bẹẹni, Oba." The girl muttered as she used her lapa to soak up what she could. Mofeyisade ran to her with more pieces of cloth to help.

"Oba." A woman emerged from the room. "You have a son."

Oba Bode rushed into the room. Ade sat in the bed drenched in sweat nursing her baby. Ade smiled as she rubbed the baby's wrinkly face with her curled fingers. She hummed to him like her mother hummed to her. She ignored Oba Bode as he walked to the bed's side. He grabbed the baby from her arms cradling the head with his large palm. He held the baby in the air as he walked to the window. It was the most gentle Ade had seen him.

The baby wailed at the top of his lungs.

"Why is he crying? Doesn't he know he has nothing to worry about," Oba Bode said.

"Maybe because you disturbed his first feeding like you disturb most things naturally," Ade said.

Oba Bode ignored her. He sat on the window sill and began to tell the baby about his wonderful future as heir to the throne. "I'll teach you about war, about how beautiful it is to watch your enemy fall at your feet. No one can conquer your father. No one will be able to conquer you." Oba Bode grinned at the crying child.

In her mind, Ade tried to figure out all the ways to combat Bode's teachings. She prayed Bode would be unamused to spend time with the child.

After his patience wore out Oba Bode softly cussed at the child for its cries. "Kings don't cry," he said as he rose to take the baby back to Ade. After he placed the baby back in her arms, he turned to the midwife and asked, "How long before she's ready to carry again?"

Ade hid her worry behind a tiresome smile.

"It'll be about eight weeks. But, it's suggested to

give a bit more time so the mother is strong in health and the baby is done nursing." The old woman eyes pierced the floor.

He turned to Ade. "You have no more than the eight weeks before I come to you for another."

Ade nestled the baby in her breast, rubbing his head softly while thinking about the day he was created.

"I sent for Oju. He should be here in a couple of days. After you meet with him, you'll make the people comply with their duties at the mines," Oba Bode said as he left.

The midwife placed a small basket near the bed for the baby. "My queen, I won't be far away. Let me know when you want me to take the child so you can rest," she said as she left the room.

Ade laid the baby next to her in the bed and wrapped him in beautiful red and gold blankets. She laid on her side, holding her head up with her hand while she continued to softly stroke the baby's face. The warmth of his face against her finger brought tears to her eyes. It reminded her of the warmth she felt in his true father's arms.

"Let me tell you about your father. He could be wise as a hundred old men when he wasn't joking. He had a strength his brother will never learn in this lifetime. And he was loving to everyone he met. That was the type of man Omoba Sakin Adesine was. That's the type of man you will be, so help me Olódùmarè." Tears hit the bed before she hummed the baby and herself to sleep.

Oba Bode barged into a room on the other side of the aafin. The servant women were giggling as they played in each other's hair, relaxing from a day's work. They fell silent when he entered, with their eyes focused on the floor and motionless.

"Leave us," Oba Bode commanded.

All of the women bounced off each other as they scattered out of the room except Mofeyisade who walked over to a table and poured two cups of wine. She pressed her breasts into his sternum. Her hand brushed his thigh after she handed him a cup.

He grabbed her by the back on her neck and brought her face up to his to kiss her. He enjoyed being with Mofeyisade. She accepted his aggressive behaviors with softness. She didn't find what he did repulsive. She fantasized about watching his maddening power decide the fate of millions of people. She thought if thousands were sacrificed for the good of the bloodline and the security of the people, then so be it. He never asked her. Many words were absent throughout the frequent visits. He preferred it that way as they moved in sync.

~

On the ninth day, Oju arrived to perform the baby's naming ceremony. Excitement exuded from Ade's face as Oju walked through the aafin's doors. Long, red and white garb flowed like ribbons. Three young men dressed in white followed him. Each student carried something: one carried his divining bag, the other pulled a goat and the last held a turtle in one hand and a snail in the other.

A white, glistening smile appeared above his long, salt and pepper beard. He stretched out his arms to hug Ade. Oju held her shoulders as he kissed her forehead. The hairs tickled her brows. Oju ignored Oba Bode standing in a nearby corridor watching them. He gently rubbed his curled, aged finger against the sleeping baby's soft cheek. The child smiled as he nestled closer to his mother's breasts.

Oba Bode was infuriated when the terms of Oju's visit reached him. He agreed not to interfere. A guest in his aafin, even for a few hours, shouldn't be able to dictate the visit. Vexation aggrandized when Ade proudly handed the baby to Oju. She frowned and argued with him whenever he asked to see the boy.

Palm wine coated Oba Bode's stomach before he prompted the servant to pour more into his cup. He watched Oju set up his divining tools and chant incantations before casting his opele to read the destiny of the child.

"Hmph," Oju grunted after he casted his opele three times. "This child's a king indeed. I can tell you now, he returns from his father's side and is a brilliant child. But, if ebo's not made he'll suffer at the hands of a demon at a young age." He paused to listen for the child's name. After he heard and confirmed the name Oju smiled. "The boy's name is Amoyi."

Ade smiled and listened intently to her son's prescriptions and destiny. The students packed Oju's tools after the reading while he cuddled the newborn and praised only its mother for its beauty in front of Oba Bode. Annoyed by their interactions, Oba Bode left the old friends to find more entertaining endeavors.

Oju pulled Ade aside by her elbow. He made sure Tekun was out of range before he spoke. "Sakin's son is beautiful." Ade's eyes widened. "Amoyi's ebo will reunite him with his father."

Ade's eyebrows furrowed. "Sakin's still alive? How will I find him?" Ade tried hard to contain the excitement in her voice.

"Do the ebo and be patient. When you do find him understand he has changed. But, don't forget he loves you." Oju finished as Tekun walked nearby. "Your son will grow to be a fine ruler like his father."

Everyone proceeded to the naming ceremony.

Guests sang the Jojolo song, pleading for the mother to come and reveal the face of their newborn arèmo. When Ade left the aafin's walls, the singing grew louder. Ade danced with the baby in her arms all the way through the capital and back to the aafin where she sat on her throne for the rest of the ceremony.

Iyalase appeared as an old woman amidst the guests dressed in a shiny white attire and a gele wrapped around her head about as tall as her. Oju stood at the front conducting the ceremony. He saw Iyalase and nodded. He walked to the table where his divining chain laid and cast to make sure he wasn't missing anything. Everything was fine. Iyalase arrived to bless the child.

Oju returned his attention to the ceremony giving the child a fingertip of water because water has no enemies and can take any form, palm oil for a smooth life, honey for a sweet life, pepper for a zestful life and liquor to know the fire of life. Everyone said a prayer for the child's wellbeing afterwards. While everyone prayed Ade whispered the secret name of the child that only she would know. When the child grew responsible enough, he would learn it and never tell. People close to Ayaba Ade were asked to give a name to the child, a medicine to urge him to become a person of great character. By the end of the ceremony the child became Arèmo Amoyi Kofi Kalejaye Eniola Adesine. Oju led the song that included all the names of the child.

A few weeks later, Ade travelled about the kingdom of Jefe with Amoyi. Each village received the child with songs and gifts. Tekun advise Oba Bode and the queen against the journey since they acquired many enemies. Longing to escape, Ade convinced the oba that anyone willing to attack the son of the king is looking for his soul to be banished into the realm of no return. Stroking Oba Bode's ego helped. He let her go with Essien to keep watch.

Meedogun

Sakin attached himself to the Balogun family over the years. He enjoyed acting as a son, husband and father; however, he longed to return home to see Ade again. He wanted to fetch her and bring her to the compound to live with him in peace. Some days he started to walk off into the woods to go back home to find her. He stopped when he found Kisi following him or when Tose called him for a game of ayo. That's how he spent most of his days after his chores, playing ayo with Tose while Kisi watched and listened to them talk about success and failures in life and war.

"It's not about how many strikes you can make. It's about making the most crippling ones." Tose coached Sakin who played like he was playing against his brother, unmethodical. Tose told Sakin to think harder about his moves. To Sakin's surprise, he began to win over time. Tose joked that Sakin was his lucky charm because the village hadn't seen an attack in over four years.

Many of Sakin's free afternoons were spent watching the Owura men wrestling in the center of the village. Real matches happened at the end of the week. Serious men had adahunse make amulets to be worn during the matches. The men most protected by those amulets won. When they won, their adahunse received praise and more clients.

Amulets intrigued Sakin. He studied them and decided to make one for himself. Sakin asked Tose who was the strongest alagbede in the village.

Sakin visited Fela's compound on Tose's advice. He admired the blacksmith's beautiful body of work as he caressed the smooth iron with his fingertips, listening to the 'ting' as his fingers jumped into the air off the blade. Fela fashioned an iron ring for Sakin while he recited to Ogun, the God of war. On his way home, he stopped by the market to purchase some red cloth from the market. He asked Morayo to sew the red cloth into a small pouch.

The night Morayo finished, he sat by a fire towards the back of the compound. He recited the incantations he learned as a boy at the Sango temple with Oju. He placed the ring into the bag during his final verse of recitation. He heard small rumblings in the sky as gray clouds formed. When he finished tying the string he tossed the bag into the fire. Sakin smiled at his achievement the next morning when he saw the bag still intact among the ashes as if nothing happened to it.

~

Villagers placed bets and cajoled as the contenders' bodies clashed like rams butting heads. The wrestlers tussled within the circle of spectators until one stuck his foot behind the other's foot and slammed the opponent on the ground. Blood splattered from their mouths as they were struck by shoulders. Many times, noses broke from the pressure of head butts. Young boys imitated the fights within the crowd. The crowd cheered as valuables were exchanged in bets. Women perched their backs as the sun beat against their breasts as the victor walked pass.

Doye was the best wrestler for years. His weight and stature was like a bull. Medicine was embedded into his skin. His face was deformed from many battles and wrestling challenges: a broken nose, split bottom lip that healed into the shape of a deep valley, and a broken eye socket that caused his eye to droop.

"Doye's always the first to go to war and the last to leave the field," Tose once told Sakin as they watched a match.

Women adored him because of his massive strength. Children emulated him, praying that if they start now they'd prove to be a warrior like him when called to battle. When Doye entered the ring, his opponent was sure to be knocked unconscious for days. Some men even died.

"Ta ni alagbara emi?" Doye lifted his large arms in the air as he slowly spun around. "Who's more powerful than me?" he asked as a man was being dragged from the ring.

"Emi ni," Sakin shouted through the crowd. "I

am."

The crowd gasped as Doye turned around to see who challenged him. He became amused when a man of smaller stature than him appeared from the crowd.

"Are you crazy, Baba Sakin?" Kisi pulled on Sakin's buba. Sakin smiled.

"Bẹẹni, you're crazy," Doye laughed. "This man thinks he can beat Doye. He's the size of Doye's baby finger." He held his pinky in comparison.

Sakin took off his buba, folded it and handed it to Morayo. He took his ring out of the red pouch and placed it on his right ring finger.

"Are you sure about this Sakin?" Morayo questioned.

"It's only sport. Give the man a chance." Tose said as he rubbed his beard amused by his new friend's wager.

"Doye could kill you," Kisi said.

Sakin bent down as he chuckled. "Kisi, no one's going to kill anyone. But, you can wish me luck." He smiled as she nodded.

"You better hope the adahunṣe who gave you that is good," Kisi said.

"I had it made and infused it with magic myself."

Kisi's eyes grew with wonderment like when Sakin told her stories around the fire at night. Morayo and Tose shifted a bit as they stood next to Sakin with concern settled on their face.

"How did you learn to do that?" Morayo asked.

"I learned as a boy."

"Like the prince in the stories," amazement permeated Kisi's voice.

Sakin nodded and stood up. He grabbed Morayo's hand and gave it a soft squeeze. "I'll be fine." He winked before entering the fighting ring.

Doye slipped his thumbs in his waist belt as he walked forward. When they met in the middle, the crowd could see Doye towered over Sakin. Doye was wider too. Sakin was tall as far he was concerned, about six foot five. However, Doye was well over seven feet tall which was more than Bode.

"You have something to prove to your family,

little one." Doye contained his laughter.

"No," Sakin simply answered.

"Then why do you come to greet death?"

"You're not death. I've seen that before. You're a man that I'll make bow to me."

Doye laughed hysterically at the idea. "Doye bows to no man."

"Oh, you will bow."

Doye bent over to meet Sakin at eye level and pointed his finger to the base of his jaw. "Give me your best."

Sakin curled his fist tightly before it sped into Doye's jaw. Doye felt his skin open as blood streamed down his neck and dripped onto the dirt. He looked at Sakin in bewilderment. The crowd gasped at the shocking sight. Tose smiled as he rubbed his beard.

Doye's fist jolted for his competitor's chin. Sakin jumped back. Doye missed. Doye charged at Sakin. Sakin evaded by stepping aside. Then he back flipped to create more distance between them. Doye charged again with his head down like a raging rhino. When

Doye was close, Sakin leaped into the air over Doye causing him to fall flat on his face. Sakin landed firm like a leopard jumping out of a tree.

The audience feverishly placed bets split between this stranger and the prized fighter. Morayo listened to women gasp and talk about the handsome Sakin.

"That's my mom's friend." Kisi loudly interjected making Morayo blush as women smacked their lips with jealousy.

The sand colored Doye's black skin with freckles of red from the long slide. He rose slowly, winded from his fall. Sakin's knee flew into Doye's chest when he turned around. The people hadn't seen an evasive yet effective fighting style. They were used to grappling and punches. They watched as Doye's size failed him against the flying man who struck out of nowhere like a snake.

Doye grabbed his chest as he landed on the ground. He rose again this time with a fist full of sand that he flung into the air when Sakin came near. Anticipating the move, Sakin flipped backwards. Doye hastily walked towards Sakin to catch him before he landed.

Sakin quickly sat down and swiped Doye's long legs tripping him. The giant landed on his back. Sakin stood up and tried to stomp Doye's gut. Doye caught Sakin's foot and flung Sakin into the air.

Doye got up and ran to catch Sakin before he landed. Doye punched Sakin's chest. He felt his wrist crack like he was hitting a tree. He grabbed his limp wrist and tried to head butt Sakin. Sakin stepped backwards and Doye landed on one knee with his head bowed. Sakin forced his knee to Doye's chin and knocked him unconscious.

The crowd stood in disbelief. They had a new victor. The fight manager hesitated to enter the ring. Doye's body refused to move. The crowd slowly started cheering the name of their new hero.

Tose entered the ring before the organizer. He walked up to Sakin. "Greet your new champion, Sakin!" Tose raised Sakin's arm into the air. Kisi ran into the ring cheering and jumping all over Sakin.

The people began to cheer louder. Winners of bets saw richness fall into their hands. Women tossed flowers into the ring. Children clustered around Sakin asking him to train them. They imitated his leaps around each other.

The fight manager entered the ring to greet Sakin. "You're favored by the Gods to win against this brute."

"I am a child of Sango," Sakin announced proudly.

"The sky god?" The old man's eyes smiled with familiarity. He remembered his younger years before he came to this town for refuge after his home was destroyed.

"Bẹẹni. Because of Sango I live," Sakin answered. "You know of Sango?"

"Bẹẹni. My baba and his baba worshipped the Thunder God."

"So you worship him too?" Sakin was excited to find someone else who worshipped Sango in the village.

"Yes, I have a space in my home for him." The old man rubbed his beard for a moment. "You should come by tomorrow. I will throw a feast for you."

"We should throw a wide festival for him and his God." Tose interrupted. "The harvest is coming soon. We could do it then."

The old man smiled. "That's a wonderful idea."

"Wa, ore mi." Tose placed his hand on the old man's shoulders. "Let us work out the details, my friend," he said as they walked away.

Doye awaken by a splash of water. He was unaware of the events going on around him. His concerned entourage helped him to his feet. They swung his big arms around their shoulders and walked off.

"Little flying man," Doye responded when his comrades asked him if he remembered anything.

Morayo walked past Sakin's new fans. She kissed Sakin on his cheek while she eyed the woman crowding around him. "I shall fix the champion a large meal." She grabbed him by the hand and guided him past the villagers who followed them until they reached the compound wall then their new admirers slowly scattered back to their lives.

Merindilogun

The villagers of Owura gathered like bees, busily moving about with offerings to the Earth for her seasonal generosity. They always celebrated the harvest festival with amusement, not only in Owura and Jefe, but throughout the continent. Everyone was connected by the basic principle of Earth as mother, providing for her children as she had done for their iyas and babas.

In Owura, however, they met this year's festival with even more exuberance than before. War was absent for almost six years since their new guest through Tose arrived. During this time the wounds of their men healed, new life was birthed and more amiable visitors stumbled upon their village and stayed. Fathers prepared their daughters for young and old suitors. The market place grew busy with fathers trading their harvest's surplus for livestock to give their sons' prospect brides' families.

Traveling herdsmen came with more livestock and sold out before they left. Many of them stayed to enjoy the abundance of Owura. Some of them were given wives.

Dresses were made, jewelry was crafted to adorn necks, wrists, stomach and ankles. Chickens, goats and cows were offered to the family's Ancestors, along with their favorite foods and drinks, to honor them and gain their blessings. The wealthiest ate for days.

Trees were planted in a grove within the compounds to ensure stability. Seeds were treated and stored to ensure abundance for the next season. Although they knew they could never replace what they took from the earth, the principle still remained the same, whatever is taken out must be put back.

For once in a long time, no one spoke of death. Every member of the family, young and old, were there to commemorate their Ancestors. Agans of vibrant patterns and colors were prepared to dance within days at the annual clan procession.

Tose found this time to be a curse and a blessing.

He was glad his people enjoyed a fruitful year yet, it
sadden him that he had very little family. Sakin noticed
this perplexity within his friend. While Sakin made an
agan for his Ancestors, he listened to the drunken Tose
pour his soul into a song about his fallen sons.

"What does a man have if he has no family at all?
If he has slain sons and barren daughters,
And a house without laughter?"

Morayo would respond to her father-in-law with
an epistle of hope.

"He has everything in life,
If his sons were slain with honor,
And his daughters affixed with more children,
Who in turn brings laughter and redemption."

Over dinner one evening Sakin inquired about
the little ancestral work Tose did during the season.
Morayo explained. The day after her husband died the
compound was engulfed by flames. Tose's spirit barely
recovered the devastating loss.

"He couldn't understand why a good man could
be so cursed," a tear fell from Morayo's eye as she won-

dered the same thing. Why would a man who honored his mothers and fathers and fought to protect their way of life be so damned.

Begrudgingly, Sakin ate his dinner as he remembered Oju once illuminated such situations for him. "Usually, proper ebos weren't made for a lineage at one point in time," Oju drew smoke from his pipe before he continued. "So the children bear the burden of their forefathers. The Gods asks us to do something today and we do it with faith, unknowing that it's for our great-great-grandchildren's protection. Or we neglect it leaving that child in misery. That's why we always obey because no one ever knows. Only Ifa knows the beginning to the end."

The next day after having a dream, Sakin purchased more fabric and asked for Morayo's help in constructing agans for Tose's Egungun. He prayed with each stitch that his friend found redemption.

Tose laid around most of the time drinking palm wine after he performed various duties throughout the village. As the chief and an elder, he was sought out for the approval of unions among the older families in the village and helped plan clan processions. He opted out of the processions this year. He couldn't raise himself out of his depression to even hear what his Towiyo were saying.

After dinner with Morayo and Kisi, Sakin returned to his abode and sewed by candlelight with Morayo's company after Kisi fell asleep. Sometimes Sakin joined Tose to drink and mourn the death of his mother and father. When Tose told Sakin his family wouldn't participate in the procession Sakin was smitten with anger. They argued. Sakin felt Tose should take a more active role in the reinstitution of his family's agans, in their Ancestor worship in general. Tose warned Sakin to stay out of his family's affairs.

"I am a well respected man, Sakin," Tose tried to further explain. "But a very poor man in many lights."

Sakin knew Tose wasn't being wise, but looked from his friend's vantage anyway. Many of Tose's daughters were married off already. Many of his sons were dead except three young boys who Tose feared would lose their lives once adulthood dawned on them and war sieged the village.

"Ore mi, you're not poor. You're rich and don't even know it. Your sons still fight with you. You're chief of this village. Everyone looks to you for what to do next."

"Bẹẹni, Sakin. But, my heart's still heavy with loss. And I sometimes I feel the disappointment of my wives." Tose rose and walk away.

~

The week progressed with offerings to the Ancestors, the Earth and Orisa Oko, the God representing the principle of going beyond your station in life towards something better. Sakin worked on the agans. On the last day of the Ancestor processions, Tose and his family sat on a raised stage to watch the last big parade. Families marched with their agans and masks. They sang and dance. They recited beautiful poems illustrating their lineage.

People began to leave after the last family of the parade to head back to their compounds to prepare for the big village celebration. Drums pounded. Everyone's heart leaped because the beat was similar to that of a coming raid. They reseated after they heard a familiar voice within the grove. It was the voice of one of Tose's slain sons.

"Who am I to my father,
If I don't die a warrior for him?
Who am I to my mother,
If I don't fight for the one who birthed me?
Who am I to my brother,
If I don't protect him?
Who am I to my people,
If I stand by watching them be killed and become slaves?"

Sakin walked down through the grove of hills followed by drummers whose hands couldn't be seen as they hit the drums like vipers. Tose rose when he saw Sakin. Morayo's eyes began to swell with tears for what this stranger, turned friend, did for her father-in-law.

The first Egungun dancing behind Sakin made everyone gasp. Mothers placed their hands over their children's eyes so they didn't see the fierce sight of the mask with two large bull horns with red tips as if it were dripping blood. As the Egungun got closer the crowd saw it was blood. Three large panels; one red, one green and one black swung and revealed two machetes cutting nearby branches to pieces.

"I am Ajigunwa Balogun, son of Tose Balogun
I died for my father yet remain immortal.
I fight for my mother because she's my portal.
I protect my brother as he protects me.
I stand up for my people because they are me."

Five different Egunguns appeared after him, each different in style and color. One walked high above the others draped in supreme white cloth. Another looked as if it had six hands each holding a weapon. A long mask with sharp teeth painted red followed by another strung solely with cowrie shells. The last one had a purple cloth with a long beaded green and black vest and a tall cowrie crown mounted above its mask.

They each announced themselves, their lineage and the same epitaph.

"I am Osaremi Balogun, I fight for you, Baba."

"I am Rotimi Balogun, I fight for you, Iya."

"I am Ibiyemi Balogun, I fight for you, Iyawo."

"I am Abiodun Balogun, I fight for you, Omo."

"I am Ikusaanu Balogun, I fight for you, my eniyan."

Tose's heart swelled as he heard the voice of his sons. They told him don't feel depressed about their physical form but rejoice. The village still stands because of their sacrifice.

Everyone rose from their seats to salute Egungun and dance. Anyone who doubted Tose or believed his family cursed was corrected at that moment. They realized Tose and his family did more for them than they've done for themselves.

The Egunguns danced towards Tose. They stood in a line and saluted him. Their mothers cried. Abiodun, the one strung with nothing but cowrie shells, greeted his wife Morayo with a bow. He took a line of cowrie shells and tied it into a necklace. He handed it to Sakin for him to drape his daughter's neck.

"Adupe, baba," Kisi said as she bowed her head.

They all danced until they reached the Balogun compound. They were followed by a large crowd. When they entered the compound each went to a different corner. Some dug holes in the earth the height of a man with their weapons. Abiodun went to the house he shared with his wife and stood motionless outside. Osaremi, the tall one draped in white, stood outside of the Balogun compound. The others disappeared into the hole they dug without a trace that they were there before.

Sakin walked to Tose and his family. "You feed Osaremi everyday. You sit and talk with him often. This is my gift to you, my friend. Since you have done so much for me."

Tose reached out to Sakin shoulders then embraced him as if he were his own son.

Metadilogun

The Balogun Egungun procession lingered on people's tongues during the village's harvest celebration. Great anticipated weddings were overshadowed by the event. Some families grew jealous of Tose's family procession. They forgot that all blessings from the Ancestors were sacred and were to be honored.

Everybody brought their compound party to the main communal area where they held the weekly wrestling matches. They danced. They drank. They sang and drummed. Children played. Others children snuck away with Kisi to see her father's shrine in front of her home. Many of the adults walked to where Tose and his family were seated to greet them and pay their respect. They were given gifts, money and wife prospects for their young sons who stood tall with warrior painted chests. They no longer feared their future as their father had. They embraced it. The ile Balogun was rejuvenated.

Sakin sat with the family thinking about his own kin. He wished he and his brother embraced each other as Tose's sons did. He thought about his father and missed Ade. Gloom permitted him from partaking in the festivities. When he felt overwhelmed he thought about his friend and his family's renewed joy. Morayo noticed his discontent and stayed near him. She wanted to console him. However, being around was enough for Sakin.

Screams of horror interrupted the joyful celebration. Sakin rose to investigate. Women and children ran in various directions. A small girl appeared from the bushes with a maimed leg. Sakin looked for a weapon. He found a ceremonial spear standing in front of the stage. A man ran to the girl, picked her up and ran to safety. Two leopards advanced from the bushes stalking anybody frozen with fear.

Sakin stood in front of the stage where Tose and his family sat with the other elders of the village. Morayo ran around frantic calling out for Kisi. Kisi ran behind Sakin to her mother who picked her up and ran on to the stage.

Sakin noticed Doye on the other side of the marketplace grounds with a myriad of men. Sakin motioned with his fingers for Doye to break his men up into groups of three to surround a leopard. Doye followed Sakin's gestures.

The leopards growled at the men's movement. Sakin picked up a rock and threw it at the closest leopard to distract it. The leopard ran towards him in anger. He stopped to back away when Sakin threatened him with the spear. The leopard paced, waiting for an opportunity to strike. It ignored the other leopard being ambushed by Doye and his men.

Taking advantage of its size the leopard lifted his massive paw and knocked the spear out of Sakin's hands. Sakin rolled away from the attack. The leopard decided on easier game. He proceeded towards Tose and the other elders. Sakin picked up his spear, ran towards the leopard, jumped into the air and stabbed its back. The leopard growled with pain.

Hunger pervaded the leopard, clouding its decisions. It continued towards Tose. As the leopard jumped on the stage Sakin mounted its back. He wrapped his arms and legs around the leopard, grasped his wrists and squeezed tight to cut off its airway. The leopard rose on its hind legs and fell on its back. Although Sakin felt winded from the beast's weight, he squeezed tighter.

The spear broke form the impact. Sakin grabbed the jagged piece that landed next to him. A warrior bellow flooded the dreadful air as he pierced the leopard's throat cutting its growl short.

Doye and his men grappled the other leopard distracted by the shriek of its hunting companion. It followed with a shriek of its own.

Sakin rose covered in blood. Villagers emerge from their hiding places. Lines of them prostrated before their savior. Doye and his comrades walked towards Sakin. Doye dropped to one knee and bowed his head. His friends mirrored the posture.

"I will fight for you," Doye said.

"Bẹẹni," the men uttered. "We all will."

Tose approached Sakin and bowed his head with respect. "My young brother. The one who brought my sons back and the savior of my village. I don't have but one daughter to give you to pay homage to your spirit and show the gratitude of my family." He motioned for Morayo to step forward. "She has stayed with me since the death of my son showing her true allegiance to the Balogun family. She is now yours. May she express the same allegiance to you and your family."

Sakin looked at Morayo and smiled. The thought of Ade made him hesitate. "I accept your gift." He bowed his head before he turned to the villagers. "Rise Owura. Continue your festival for you still have life among you."

Mejidilogun

Adunni's skin itched. The dry heat irritated her skin more. She resisted the urge to scratch her peeling skin as her faux husband walked past her in the courtyard. She was given many jobs around the palace. Gardening was her favorite. Although it forced her to stay outside in the heat all day, maintaining the beauty of the Jama's prized mosque and palace, she enjoyed the solitude that came with it. She daydreamed as she tended to the desert plants.

The shock of becoming a slave waned years ago. Her anger never ceased. She wasn't angry with the Emir and Saddiq anymore. At least, not as much as she was with her brother for never coming to check on her. She was the Emir and Saddiq's prisoner, but to her brother, it was like she didn't exist anymore.

Her threats of Bode coming and taking all of the Jama's land fell on laughing ears. No one was coming back for her. So, she tried to devise a new plan- get close to Saddiq, which was impossible. He was either with one of his growing number of wives or at the mosque or playing emissary for his father. When he did come in contact with her, it was cold and distant.

Today, he was showing off some young bride. He paraded one of his wives in front of Adunni every chance he got. Inside, Adunni laughed. The women were taller than Adunni and thin. At least, that's what they appeared to be underneath all the garb. Adunni was fuller in her breasts and hips. The women were beautiful, but none were as beautiful as her. Even with her ragged clothes and years of torment she felt her beauty untouched. The women that he paraded also never bore him a child. Adunni certainly laughed at that because the small boy sitting next to her was an identical image of his father who never claimed him, the Emir.

Her first child, a girl, born several months after she arrived, was taken from her. She thought the child was dead until she found out later the child was sold.

She never found out where the child dwelled. Her second child, another girl, was taken from her and given to Saddiq's oldest wife because they had trouble with conception. The father was unknown because Saddiq let his soldiers do whatever they wanted to Adunni. That was until they bragged about her to him then he had to have her for himself.

Saddiq laid with Adunni many nights enjoying the pleasure she gave him, untamed by the prudent protocols forced on women in his society. Not all women were like that, this Adunni knew for sure as a slave that travelled about the palace. Many of them were very traditional. Others, however, just enjoyed the touch of a man.

From what Adunni knew Saddiq was sterile. This was discovered when his third wife had a baby by another man. Her infidelity went unnoticed because another one of Saddiq's wives got pregnant by her lover around the same time. The women paraded the children around as if they belonged to him.

Adunni was still an outcast among everybody.

Even the slaves rejected her because she was from Jefe and apart of a royal bloodline. Most of them were born slaves with no opportunity to change their destiny. Adunni paid no attention to any of it. She occupied her mind with fantasies of escape and devised plans on how to get her children back. To make sure her daughter knew her, Adunni visited her every evening.

A few days later, Saddiq came to the slave's room to see Adunni. This time he brought beautiful clothes.

"What's this for?" Adunni asked.

"Your brother's sending his counsel to check on you."

Adunni looked at him suspiciously. It's been too long for her to believe someone was coming for her. Then her heart fluttered. If it's Essien she might finally get away.

"If you tell the councilman of your true living arrangements then I'll be forced to slaughter him and your children," Saddiq threatened. "For the next week you will act as my wife."

"Do your other wives know?"

"Don't question me about my wives. All you need to know is what'll happen if you don't oblige." Saddiq left the room.

Adunni spread the clothes over the bed. She liked the patterns. "I look good in blue," she said to herself as she shrugged her shoulders.

The other slaves entered the room. She enjoyed their jealous eyes as she held the clothes against her body. Pretending was something she would do if it got her home quicker.

As the week progressed, Adunni appeared more beautiful than before. She was elegant, a trait Saddiq refused to understand because of the people she came from. He was taught to hate her people because they practiced a religion his god abhorred. He was very young when his father adopted the religion of Islam and proclaimed it the true religion of the Jama. His knowledge about the traditional Deities were replaced with Allah. If anybody mentioned Hevioso, Dada Sogé or Iya Ponda they were beaten inches to death. Some nights he heard Adunni praying. He was ready to beat her if she mentioned any foreign name. His impulses were curbed when he heard her say the name of her Ancestors. What he didn't know was that praying to the Ancestors was the same as praying to the Deities because all bloodlines tie back to their true source.

Essien arrived for the banquet dinner on the eve of the couple's sixth year anniversary. Adunni was surprised to see Essien with more soldiers than she had when she arrived. The person who really stuck out in Essien's company was his son, Ode.

Adunni's heart stopped beating as her eyes gazed over the man she first loved. Even though he was tall before he was taller now. He was thin, sticking true to the ile Akata men's trait. His muscles, however, complimented his thin frame. He tried to grow a beard from the coarse patches Adunni saw on his face and neck, but it was unsuccessful. She wanted to believe her eyes. She wanted to reach out and touch him. She knew anger and confusion would boil out of the Emir and Saddiq since women were forbidden to touch a man in public, especially a married one.

"Bawo ni?" Ode asked as he approached her by the food table. "How are you?"

"Se alafia ni." She replied breathlessly. "I am fine." It was him as far as she could tell in the brightly lit room. "What are you doing here?"

"I am training to take my father's place. He brings me along to various villages within Jefe and outside of the kingdom, what's left that is. Your brother has been on a rampage."

Adunni didn't care to know what her brother was up to since it wasn't about saving her. "That's good. I mean the training to take your father's place even though Akata men live a very long time. So you won't see your duties pan out until late in life."

Ode nodded. "You were always observant," he smiled. "I guess until then I have to look like I'm important. But, you, soon-to-be queen of the Jama. If I understand correctly from Oba Bode's arrangements."

Adunni smiled. "Yes, if it were a perfect world."

Ode's smile erased. He looked deeply into Adunni's eyes. He raised his hand to cup her cheek.

"Don't." Adunni softly place her hand on his hand before it reached her face. "I am happy with my new life." She half smiled before she walked away.

Ode watched her. After years of knowing her, he knew something was amiss. He grabbed a purple orb and plopped into his mouth. He chewed hard as he thought about the nights he spent with her. If it were true, if she was happy, she would deny him tonight. That's what he repeated to himself as he walked down the halls later that night. He was perplexed when he found she wasn't sleeping in the room they said she'd be in. Instead he entered the female slaves' room and found her nursing a plump little boy too young to be his child.

"What are you doing in here?" Adunni questioned. "You have to leave now before someone finds you here."

"Why are you in here? Why aren't you with your husband?"

Adunni sighed. She placed the sleeping child on her bed and pulled the covers up to his chin. She folded her arms when she turned to face Ode.

"Everything you see is a lie. My brother placed me here to be a spy. The Emir and his son didn't want me. They made me a slave. They were upset with the broken agreement between my brother and them. They took my first born, our child, and sold her. They took my second girl and put her with Saddiq's first wife."

"And this one?"

"They let me keep him."

"We have to go. I have to get you out of here."

"If we leave they'll find us and kill us."

"But if we make it back home to tell your brother. I think that's a chance we should be willing to make."

Adunni thought about it. She knew how to get in and out of the palace. She only stayed because the risk was too much with two small children, but with Ode she had a chance.

"Ok. But I have to get my daughter. I'm not leaving her here. She should be in her room."

Ode looked outside the room before he motioned for Adunni to follow. She held the child close to her bosom under the cloak. She led the way to her daughter's room. She softly opened the door. The girl was there sound asleep. Ode picked the girl up and followed Adunni down the halls and out the back of the palace through the empty kitchen. They stopped by the stables to get Ode's horse. They sped off into the night outside of the sand walls.

Mokandinlogun

Saddiq's first wife roamed the halls before she checked on her daughter. This was something she did that nightly before bed. When she discovered the girl was absent from her bed she shrieked.

"My daughter's gone!" She ran out into the halls, yelling with tears. She flew to Saddiq's room to find him gone. She ran to a guard who took her to Saddiq who was with Essien trying to keep up appearances.

Saddiq's wife explained that on her normal routine she found their daughter out of her bed. Saddiq ran to the slave quarters and found the slave girls giggling while they chatted. No one had saw Adunni for a few hours. Essien watched Saddiq check the bed for clues. Essien's suspicions were confirmed, Adunni was Saddiq's slave, not his wife.

"Where's your son?" Saddiq asked Essien.

"I'm sure he's resting in his room."

Saddiq and Essien ran to the room and found it empty. Saddiq turned to his guards and ordered them to search the palace and the surrounding areas. He pulled the commander aside, the true father of Adunni's second child, and whispered in his ear. The guards left to carry out his orders. Saddiq took Essien back to the room where they were found and waited while he consoled his wife.

Adunni and Ode moved without hesitation. They knew they needed to get as far away before day broke because once the sun rose there was nowhere to hide. They wouldn't reach the forest for another three days. They arrived at a village before day broke. They hid in the place where visitors stayed to rest. Ode purchased a room for them. They stayed there until night fell and continued their journey.

Adunni spoke with Ode of an alternate plan to enact if they were caught. She knew the possibility of her children making it back to Jefe were slim. They agreed to pay a female worker a generous sum to keep the girl until either one of them returned or the woman met a thin man of dark complexion who looked like Ode. They left Essien's name. The boy was too young to stay behind.

The girl, who Adunni called Abioye, was confused even though she knew Adunni. Adunni spent many nights with her after her mother visited her and talked to her about who she was. Abioye didn't have strong Jama features. She looked like Adunni. She listened to Adunni's stories of a kingdom called Jefe. She trusted Adunni.

Abioye was a small girl no more than five years old. She was old enough to watch the people around her. She heard the slaves gossip about her true origin and negative things her mother's sister wives said to her mother when she was present. Abioye thought the woman who stayed in her room with the boy at night was telling the truth. She stayed with the stranger after her true mother kissed her goodnight and tried to pray the way she taught her.

Jama soldiers didn't spare anytime to rest. They rode until they caught up with Adunni and Ode at the forest edge. The Jama soldiers surrounded them.

"Give us the girl," the commander shouted.

"I don't have her," Adunni yelled back. "I just have my son."

A Jama soldier pulled Ode off the horse. Adunni cradled her son closer to her bosom muffling his cries. The soldiers stood around Ode beating him. When there was no sight of the little girl the commander unmounted his horse and walked to Ode. He held Ode by his hair.

"Where is she?" the commander asked Adunni.

"I don't know what you're talking about. I only grabbed my son."

The commander pulled out his saber and held it to Ode's neck. "Are you willing to let him die?"

Adunni silently cried. She refused to look at Ode. She heard a thump and screamed when she saw Ode's head roll near the horse's hooves.

"Take her to the yuvo. We have no use for her anymore," the commander said to two soldiers. "Sell her and the child."

"You'll be selling the Emir's son!" Adunni shouted, trying to evade the horrid destiny.

"All of the Emir's sons are within the palace,
slave," the commander retorted as he wiped his blade
clean.

"What about the little girl?" a soldier asked.

"Search every village along the way back. She has
to be somewhere."

The soldiers ordered to escort Adunni pulled her
and the child off the horse. She stumbled with sadness
and exhaustion during the long trek to the coast. The
soldiers sold her and the child once they reached the
coast. She was caged with the other people. She cursed
herself and her Ancestors for the events that happened
to her. She didn't want to pray because what good had
that gotten her. However, as tears flowed from her eyes,
she prayed anyway.

The commander searched the villages on the way
back and came up empty handed. He met with Saddiq
and the Emir who kept Essien close. The commander
placed a bloody bag on the table and opened it enough

to show Ode's head.

"Do you know what you've done?" Essien asked.

"Tell your oba the war never ended."

Essien rose and left the palace with his son's body.

Ogun

Three weeks after the harvest festival, Sakin and Morayo's wedding took place. Sakin built a home of his own within the Balogun compound. Morayo and Kisi abandoned their home to live with him. A plot of land was given to Sakin to plant and harvest whatever he chose.

When Sakin and Morayo entered the hut, he sat down and waited for her to bring a bowl of warm water to wash his feet. She slowly sprinkled water down his soles. She rubbed the water into his feet then grabbed a handful of water to bathe them again. She dried his feet with new white linen given as a ceremonial gift and took some lavender oil, another wedding gift, and rubbed it into his feet. After she rubbed in the oil, she got up to fetch another gourd of warm water. She sat beside him. Sakin rose to sit at her feet and began to do the same.

When finished Sakin poured the water out in the back of his new home. Upon his return he found Morayo naked except for the blue and white beads her former mother-in-law strung for her. The beads wrapped her like a vest before encircling her waist. Sakin admired his wife. He found beauty in her before, but it was more of a friendship. He never wanted to overstep his boundaries with her because he enjoyed her company and his heart still dwelled on Ade. Now he admired her as a woman. He admired her as his wife.

He removed his buba. His chest was decorated with scars from the wounds from his battle with the leopard. He slowly walked to her as she back onto their bed to sit down. With each step his desire grew. He stopped between her legs and brushed her cheek with the back of his hand. The tip of his fingers met her jawline then he cupped her cheek. She nestled her nose into his palm and kissed it. He lowered himself to his knees.

They gazed into each other's eyes as they listened

to the busy insects outside.

"I haven't been with another man since my last husband," Morayo said softly.

Sakin nodded. "I know."

"I still love him."

"Bẹẹni, I know." Sakin gently spoke.

Sakin brushed her hair before he spoke again. "I've been with many and only loved one."

Morayo nodded.

"Tonight I lay with you as my wife. A love I didn't expect to have. A woman consumed with loyalty and compassion. Friendship and love. You're mine and I love you deeper than you can imagine."

Morayo smiled. "Mo nife o, Sakin Adesine."

He kissed her. She rubbed his emblazoned scars. She leaned back on her palms as he sucked. He kissed down her navel.

"You will bear my royal seeds," he whispered to her womb.

She rubbed her palms over his freshly healed wounds from the leopard. She wanted to stay by the

Balogun's side because their son was so good to her. She wasn't his first wife, not even his second. She was the only one to have a child and the only one to stay beyond his death. Fulfilling her oath to him and his family awarded her with Sakin, the most feared man within the village, containing deeper secrets than she could know. He was a man that carried himself like a king and loved his friends as if they were his family. She fell in love with him a long time ago. Now she could express that love.

"It's my honor to bear your children," she whispered as she kissed him.

He kissed her forehead before he drifted off to sleep.

~

That night he dreamed of rolling thunder and lightning. A sea of black faces appeared before him standing on a large body of water. They were men, women and children. Some were in good health, some were sick. Some were badly injured and some were inflated like they drowned. Some weeped and some yelled with anger.

The same black skeletal spirits he saw coming for the elderly man and girl, the day of his brother's coronation, were trying to rip the souls out of the people. Most of the people fought the spirits back. Some of them let the dark spirits take their soul, falling into black ash afterwards, crumbling to the bottom of the sea.

As thunder clashed in the heavens, he saw Sango fighting with the dark being the skeletal spirits were birth from. While they fought Oya, in her whirlwind manifestation, ripped the souls out of the dark spirits grasps and tossed them into a black hole in space where Sakin saw many people dressed in white catching them.

Sakin woke up sweating. He shook the bed so much, Morayo woke up. She wiped the sweat off his forehead. He explained to her what he saw. She had no words for him. She didn't understand it. She just knew it was a powerful vision given to him by the Deities.

Morayo left the bed to fix him some tea. After

Sakin drank it, he was relaxed enough to fall back to sleep. This time he dreamed his father was handing him the crown.

Ogun Okan

Ade kept herself busy as much as possible. If she wasn't running behind Amoyi she was on business trips as the ayaba and head of commerce. She often visited her home where she got to relax from Oba Bode's tumultuous tempers. There she laughed with her sisters as her son made humorous remarks and amusing discoveries. She thanked the Gods and Goddesses her child was able to be jovial despite living in a tense household where his parent's fought about everything.

Every time she looked into Amoyi's eyes she saw Sakin's spirit. That was enough to wake her the next morning. She thought about Sakin, gazing at the walls painting memories and constructing a life she knew was unattainable at the moment. Although he was gone, having a piece of him with her, a being they created, was sufficient.

Oba Bode wanted to taint the child's good nature. He wanted to send the child through rigorous trainings of weaponry and jakuta. He would reprimand Amoyi with a punch or a kick whenever he was pleasant with the servants and citizens. "Kings should be feared not loved," Bode repeatedly stated. These occurrences ended with Ade in her husband's bedroom where she privately argued and fought with him.

"Why on Earth would you hit a child like that!" She yelled after demanding Mofeyisade leave the room.

Oba Bode rose out of the bed and wrapped his waist with a long bed sheet. He walked over to a table adorned with fruit, wine and cigars. He lit a cigar. "Come back soon and bring the girl that's fresh in age." He turned to tell Mofeyisade. "Unless of course, my wife wishes to bed her husband tonight." He chuckled at Ade's stern face. "Very well then." He sat down on a bench as Mofeyisade closed the door.

"Amoyi is only a small child. You shouldn't beat him like a dog," Ade continued.

"I will do with him as I see fit. He's my heir." A large gray cloud exited his gaped mouth. The room was thick with stale smoke. "At his age I was already fighting men twice my size. Not very long after that I was planning battles with my father and his generals."

"He's not you. He has a choice in how he wants to rule this kingdom and he will do so with…"

"With what? Love?" He laughed at the idea. "You control people with fear not love."

"No, you treat them like human beings. Not animals at your disposal. They trust in the king to protect them from invaders so they can live out their time with their families in peace. So they can worship their Ancestors and the Deities. That's the type of king he should be, like his grandfather and not some blood thirsty monster like you."

Oba Bode rubbed his wrinkled forehead. "Are you finished?" he asked as he chuckled. "He will protect the people. But, he will do so with a strong arm holding a machete."

"But, he's a peaceful child…"

"He's a weak child!" Oba Bode cut her short. "And no child of mines will be tolerated as weak even if

I have to beat him to death."

"You will not harm my child again or..."

"Or what!" Oba Bode yelled. "What Ade! You'll leave!" He rose and walked towards her with the cigar in his mouth. "That doesn't bother me," he said as he removed the cigar and held it between his fingers. "I'll just replace you with someone who's not a wench. Who makes love to her husband, her king, like bed whores." He continued to walk towards her. He smiled when she backed away. He grabbed the cloth on her shoulder and shifted it to expose her skin.

"You will not harm my child again or I'll kill you." She swatted his wrist away.

"You cannot kill me. No one can kill Oba Bode." He lifted his arms and spun around. "I am God of this land!" he shouted.

Ade turned to leave the room.

"Where are you going?" Oba Bode asked as he walked over to the table to pour himself some palm wine. Ade watched the white wine flow into the cup. She imagined his blood doing the same. "I want to sleep with my wife. I want to have another child." The notion disturbed her thoughts.

"I pray I'm barren before I bare your child," she hesitated, "again." She turned to open the door.

Bode threw the glass at the door. It shattered before her face, the liquid soiling her purple and white dress. She turned her face from the explosion. A piece of glass ripped through the skin on her neck. She shouted, "Abami O!" Thick droplets of blood dripped down her neck and over the shoulder Oba Bode uncovered. "You monster."

Oba Bode took long steps over to her. "You'll start acting as my wife!" He spun her around by her shoulder and slapped Ade across her cheek with the back of his hand. "Even if I have to take you, you'll bear another child. And I'll take you until I'm satisfied." He grabbed her by the wrist and threw her towards his bed.

"Why do you terrorize me!" Ade shouted.

Oba Bode laughed, his belly jumped with amusement. "Because my brother loved you." Ade's eyes widen at his honesty. "And to torment him further as he lays at the base of the river, you'll bear as many of my children as your body can withstand."

"Why do you hate him so much?"

"Because my father loved him more than me." He began to walk towards her. "So you'll love me more than him." He ripped the string that held her dress closed.

"I'll never willingly sleep with you." She held her dress together with her bloody hand.

"You will or I'll burn your people alive to the ground." He noticed the threat didn't move her like the times before.

"Iya! Iya!" Amoyi banged on the door. "I've been looking for you. It's time for my stories," he said as he opened the door.

"Amoyi, stop right there," she commanded with her finger.

"What's going on?" Amoyi looked at the shattered glass and wine on the floor before he saw his mother bleeding. "Baba, why did you do that!" he shouted as he ran to him with fists. He pounded the laughing oba. Hearing Oba Bode laugh harder provoked him into kicking him.

Oba Bode walked over to the table and grabbed a small carving knife. The boy followed him with his flying arms. Before Ade could grab Amoyi, Oba Bode turned around and grabbed the boy's chin with his palm as Amoyi cried for his mother.

"You will or I'll leave you with no children." He held the knife to Amoyi's throat.

"And leave yourself without an heir?" Ade challenged.

"Children can be replaced," he said as he slowly pierced the boy's neck.

"Stop!" Ade shouted when she saw blood run. "I'll do as you say."

Mofeyisade returned with Tocarra. Bode smiled at their perked exposed breasts. "I changed my mind. Take the boy to his keeper." He pushed Amoyi forward.

"Iya!" Amoyi cried. Mofeyisade walked towards him to grab the boy.

"It's okay, baby. I'll see you at sunrise, my prince," Ade tried to reassure him.

Ade removed her dress when the door closed. She listened to her son's cries fade down the hall. Oba Bode walked to her with the blade in hand. He rubbed the cold blade down the middle of her chest then around her breast.

"I'll never love you," she said.

He looked at her body then roughly grabbed her face. "That's fine." He forced her lips open with his tongue. "Just having you is enough for now." He threw her onto the bed.

Ade woke moments before him to grab the nearby knife. Oba Bode's eyes opened with red irises when she leaned up for more leverage. She plunged the blade into his chest. It broke as it tried to pierce his skin. He raised his arm and smacked her off the bed. She hit the wall. He walked over to her. While she tried to get up she found a shard of glass. She attempted to use it when he was in range. He kicked her chest. She released the makeshift weapon. He kicked her until she was unconscious.

She found herself in her room being taken care of by her servants. She asked for her son. They told her he was away with the oba on business.

Mejilelogun

Horseback riding amused Amoyi. Excitedly, he joined Oba Bode with a myriad of warriors on a business expedition. For days they rode through the forest trails until they emerged from the thicket and faced a vast blue body of water. The salty air smelled refreshing. He wondered if the people his father captured felt the same. Amoyi was told they were bad people trying to overthrow the king. His mother told him the opposite and he believed her.

Oba Bode came to speak personally with a business partner to trade gold, food and people. He wore royal red and white garbs. He unmounted his horse and walked to a pasty white man. Tekun, Amoyi and three ẹso followed him.

"Ah, I see you've been putting the guns to good use," the pasty man said.

"Bẹẹni, Jack. They work very well."

"And who's this little fella?" The man grinned revealing rotten yellow and black teeth.

"This is Arèmo Amoyi, my son," Bode said with his chest out.

"Your father's a real good man. I hope to do business with you some day." He reached out his hand.

Amoyi cleared his throat and spat in the man's face.

"Why you little…" The man lunged towards Amoyi with both hands.

Oba Bode stepped in front of Amoyi. Tekun and his men stepped forward and settle into a fight stance with the guns drawn.

"He'll be dealt with," Oba Bode said sternly. "I came here to trade in person. It has been a while."

The man looked at Oba Bode and smiled. "Alright. Step into my office." The man wiped his face cussing as he turned around to walk over the hot sand. Four tall thick sticks with a sheet of cloth draped over rising and falling in the wind acted as his office.

Oba Bode turned to Amoyi and slapped him

across the face. "You will learn respect," he said. He looked at his warriors. "Tekun and you three walk with me. The rest of you stay with the captives." He walked away with Amoyi trailing behind.

Amoyi looked at the beautiful blue water that turned white as it pounded against the sand. There were three anchored ships wading in the water. The side of them were marked with foreign letters he figured he hadn't learned yet.

There were five men seated around a fire. One turned a large pig over the fire as they drank from their cups. They laughed as a man came out of a tent with a woman blacker than Amoyi bound by her wrists with a disconnected look in her eyes. The man fixed his pants as he walked pass with her.

She was beautiful. She was tall as his mom with lips as full as hers. Her breasts were like perfect circles Amoyi practiced drawing. Her neck was long and her skin glisten from the sweat reflecting the sun. Her hips were wide and her buttocks was big.

The man walked her back to the large cage they

built to keep the captives. The men were separated from the women. The captives were mostly young men and women. They sat in the sun speaking languages unfamiliar to Amoyi. Many of them were crying. Some appeared to be praying. Others just sat there waiting.

Jack made a hissing sound after drinking from his cup when they stepped into the office.

"Good ole brandy. Here try it." The man passed Bode the small white cup. Oba Bode took the cup. He looked at the brown liquor in the cup and swirled it around a bit before he sipped it. He coughed before it finished gliding down his throat.

The man laughed at him as he grabbed the cup. "You savages don't know good liquor, even if it bit you in the ass." He sipped from the cup again and made the same hissing sound with a grunt as he sat down at his brown plank desk supported by barrels. He sat the cup on a pile of papers and a map charting the sea. He moved his navigation tools to prop his feet up. Dirt and sand flung from his black, worn boots onto the map. Some flecks flew into the cup. "What can I do for you?"

"I have lots of gold, planks of wood and freshly harvested food," Oba Bode said.

"Well, it looks like we've got a problem. Now that's fine and all, but I need more slaves. Seems like we can't get enough of them. Many of them die on the ships or jump overboard and drown. And when they get to the new world, they die within two years. My company sends me here to keep everybody stocked. See those slaves over there?" he pointed. "They'll be in the new world by spring. But that ain't nearly as many as I'm suppose to have. I worked out a deal with you. You bring me the captives from your war advancements and I'll keep you supplied with the newest weaponry on the market. Now we had a pretty good deal until you showed up here with less than fifty heads. I don't wanna make more than two trips this year. I want to spend time with my wife and kids." He stopped to read Bode's face and sipped from his cup. "Look, what are you looking to get today? Maybe, I can work something out with you. We've been doing good all these years."

"I need more guns if you want more captives. And barrels of your new brandy. That'll do well at the markets," Oba Bode spoke.

"How many are you looking to get?"

"I've added over five hundred men to my army."

The man let out a whistle. "That's a lot of guns you're asking for. What are you going to bring me in return?"

"I'll bring you enough captives to fill a fleet of three ships." Oba Bode stared at the man.

The man smiled at the idea. If he returned with that many savages he could retire from the sea for a while and enjoy his life comfortably. He could send his oldest boy to medical school and enroll the other three. He leaned back in his chair and rubbed his scruffy salt and pepper face.

"And if I don't see a return. I'll call upon my queen to send an army after you," Jack said after he contained himself.

Oba Bode's jaw clenched at the threat.

"Alright. You got yourself a deal." Jack reached

his chubby hand out. Oba Bode reached out and shook his hand.

"Hey Henry," Jack called out to a man sitting around drinking and joking around the fire.

"Yes, Captain," the man responded.

"Get these fine savages hooked up with twenty boxes of guns and fifty barrels of brandy."

"Yes, Captain." The man smiled at the large sell and ran off to the ship followed by his friends.

Metalelogun

Juice burst from the leaf between Ade's fingertips. She rubbed the slimy juice on her scarred neck while she watched Amoyi play with his cousins. Amoyi told her about the expedition when he returned with Oba Bode. She argued with Bode about taking Amoyi to the coast to trade people for guns. Oba Bode didn't care about her thoughts on the matter. Instead, he dismissed her as he looked over maps to invade another village.

Ade watched her son pick fruit from the marula tree in her family's compound. Her father chatted with her uncles as he sat on a tree stump. Her sisters braided each other hair. Ade leaned back on the tree and relaxed.

Her home village swelled over the last four generations. She told Amoyi about their Ancestors who travelled from the North. A tribe of them decided to stay in this fertile land while others continued south. They called the village Jembe. A man ten generations before her was one of the tribesman of a group called Bantu. He stayed.

They were primarily hunters. As the hunter's children grew older, they became adept traders. They travelled on the paths they made through the forest to other villages. They sold what they caught in the wild or what their wives harvested. Sometimes these hunters turned businessmen came back with beautiful stones and artwork to trade.

The forest became the entrance of the village. It was along the same river Sakin drowned in, but was far away from Jefe. Ade visited the river with her sisters and thought about Sakin while praying she'd see his spirit. She sang the same song she sang to him and now to her son. She sometimes saw Sakin across the wide river. Amoyi would jump into her lap fracturing the illusion. When finished lounging at the river, Ade and her sisters fetched river water and carried it back to their compound on their heads along the same path their foremothers walked.

Pass the trees at the entrance two men with drums and a flatten bell sat there to warn of new visitors or invaders. They never heard the call of invaders. Just the ring of visitors. Once a visitor entered they'd see rows of housing compounds as far as they could see all around them. The houses were wide cylinders with brown thatched rooftops. One couldn't see pass the large market in the middle of the city. Pass that was a large plain that many people dared not to venture into because of the large cats that hunted antelopes. Since food was always in abundance there was rarely an incident of attack in Jembe.

As the seasons changed the people watched the herds of elephants, zebras and a multitude of other animals migrate. The sight of them walking, sometimes in unison, was beautiful with the snow capped mountains as their background. It meant the rain season was coming.

Amoyi loved to visit his mother's homeland. He played with children his age, enjoyed the beautiful colors and at night listened to the various instruments permeating the dark sky. He lived in peace and harmony.

That changed. Amoyi and his mother heard explosive sounds come from the entrance of the village. His family crowded behind his mother with terror in their eyes. They knew the oba's threats. Ade tried to assure them they were merely threats.

The family, some with half braided hair, cried as they saw women screaming and running from the marketplace. The youngest cried the hardest because her mother was at the market.

Men on horses with machetes and ibons appeared. The threat was no longer idle when Ade saw Tekun in a general uniform.

"Iya, what's going on?" Amoyi asked.

"Owani, take the children and hide in the house," Ade commanded. She was sure at least her family would be spared.

Villagers ran for the forest beyond the plains to hide. Before they reached it, troops of warriors emerged shooting their guns. Jembe men got their ibons, armor and machetes out. Although an invasion never happened, the men trained were in warfare. Since they were friendly with the council in Jefe weapons were affordable. The men didn't concede as they aimed their guns and arrows at the horsemen and struck them.

No one found time to bow as the oba rode through on his black armored horse in his general attire. He rode until he reached Ade's compound, trotting over blood and maimed bodies. He found Ade and Amoyi when he arrived.

"I thought you were in Obade on business," he addressed Ade. "Well, it's best the boy sees first hand what a siege looks like."

"You promised you'd never touch my people," Ade spoke calmly.

"I have more important deals I have to keep. You have enough people here to pay my debts."

Tekun rode to Oba Bode's side. "My queen," he spoke to Ade. The title alone tormented her since she wasn't able to protect her people from her husband. He treated her more like his own slave than the queen of his kingdom.

"The number of people appear to be down, oba," Tekun said.

"Then burn the village. The people are hiding behind their pretty walls. Go to their farmlands as well, many of them are ensuring the next harvest," Oba Bode ordered.

"Bẹẹni, oba." Tekun turned the horse and kicked its sides before he rode off.

Oba Bode got off his horse. "Baba," he said to Ade's father rose to bow. Oba Bode moved the stump for a better view. He sat down and watched. He called Amoyi to his side. "You clear the land of everything. Send the people somewhere else, either to the new world or heaven. Then you build your legacy on top of it and spread your seed. One day, I will give you this faction to rule."

Ade sternly watched in horror as her people fell to the Jefe Army. The young and old were bound by their wrists as they were taken out of their homes. Their valuables burned behind them. She cried within for them while she planned revenge.

"The Ancestors never forget," Ade said as she watched her people's demise.

"Fetch me a drink, baba. This is a good showing of my new men," Oba Bode said to Dele who moved briskly as he held his stumped wrist. Bode ignored his wife's comment.

Merinlelogun

Planning to invade Jefe proved difficult. Sakin knew every road, house and corner in the capital city. However, getting inside without being murdered on sight would be impossible. Sakin convinced himself it was time, but he needed a way to ensure success since his brother increased his hoard of warriors.

He meditated by fire many nights imagining the conquest. His brother had ibons, he didn't. His brother had men trained in warfare since birth. Sakin had warriors out of necessity not birthright. To be sure of how his brother operated he needed an inside connection. His beautiful Ade came to mind. He sent a troop of messengers to retrieve her, hopeful she'd return with them.

Tose provided three messengers. These men hunted and mapped the land prior to Sakin's arrival. Sakin was found by the waterfall penetrating the sky for miles. They stayed near the river while they hiked the mountains. The men walked for days after they reached the top. They didn't stop until they noticed old women washing clothes on stones surrounded by children on the other side of the river. The river was too wide to cross at that point. They kept marching until they met a group of fishermen on boats.

Two boats responded to the Owura men's calls. The men asked about Jefe and if they were close. The men proudly announced their village was a faction of the kingdom. The messengers exposed a small pouch of cowries. The fishermen smiled and agreed to take them across the river. Once they were on the other side the fishermen told them how to enter Jefe through the forest. There was a trading path that led directly to the city. They would know because there would be many men with mules pulled cart loads of goods.

Along the path, the messengers encountered many sellers of epo, salt, pottery and dried fish. The path was a market flowing like a river. They also saw horsemen with guns watching the businessmen and checking for visitors. The men were forced to explain where they were from and what business they had in Jefe a few times.

One of the guards traveling along the path was Tekun. He took interest when he heard the men were on their way to visit the oba of Jefe. After interrogating them he decided to take them to Oba Bode himself.

"What business do you want with me?" Oba Bode asked as Tekun let the men enter after speaking with him.

Oba Bode was sitting as he watched Amoyi train in jakuta. The boy was tired and began stammering as his opponent approached him. Every time he was overtaken by the trainer Bode reprimanded him with a punch of his own.

"We have come far, Oba. Our village has heard of the riches one gains from joining your kingdom. We wish to do so," the spokesman bowed.

"Where are you from?"

"A village called Owura, several weeks south of here."

"If you join me, what's to keep me from selling you as slaves?" Oba Bode rose to walk to his desk and pour himself a drink of brandy.

The men were shocked by the statement. They expected the oba to take them on friendly terms.

"We have much to offer. We have men strong enough to join your army. We have precious stones that can only be mined on the other side of the river." The spokesman placed a bag of colorful stones on the table. "We only come to add to your wealth."

Oba Bode observed the stones with Tekun. "Fetch Ayaba Ade," he told Tekun.

The men looked at each other, confounded. They were told to bring a woman named Ade. They didn't expect her to be a queen.

Moments later, Ade appeared inside the room. Her face was sullen and hard. Lines developed around her eyes hinting the stress she was experiencing. Yet, her beauty still prevailed.

"Have you seen these stones before?" Oba Bode asked as he handed her some of the stones.

Ade weighed them in her hands. She looked at the beautiful blue, red and orange colors. She smiled at some memories she had of them.

"Bẹẹni, they're rare to come by. Some men from the south crossed the river to trade in Jembe from time to time." Her voice trembled at the thought of her village.

"How much can we get for these?" Oba Bode asked.

"They were worth ten bag of cowries each. Probably more now since no one has seen them since I was a girl."

"Yuvo would love this," Tekun chimed.

Oba Bode sat to think about the offer. "Why do you want to join my kingdom?"

"We ask for protection from invaders south of us. They raid us every harvest for these stones."

"Seems like you're worth more as miners than warriors," Oba Bode chuckled. "We shall see if I take you for that."

Oba Bode took another sip of brandy as he

looked at his map. He enjoyed the thought of expanding beyond the river. He could take more villages there
and sell the captives. His mind was so set on expanding
north to regain what his father lost. However, the South
seemed like an easy target and a way to train his new
warriors before they clashed with the Turegs and Jama
in the North.

"I'll send someone with you to see for myself if
you're useful." He motioned for Tekun to lean his ear
towards him. Tekun nodded when he was finished and
left the room. "I'll send one of my councilmen. My
most prominent one is away on other affairs at the moment."

"If it's all the same to you, we suggest Ayaba Ade
come with us since she's aware of the stones' worth," the
messenger said.

Oba Bode rubbed his chin as he pondered the
suggestion. Ade pestered him on how he handled the
child. He could use a break from her bickering and
constant acts against his life.

"Bẹẹni. I believe that would be in your favor,"

Oba Bode smiled. "Ade prepare to leave tomorrow," he commanded her.

"And what of Amoyi? He should come with me to learn about trade and acquisition."

Oba Bode nodded. "He shall go. He may prove to be a better businessman than a warrior." He shook his head as he looked at the thin boy.

Amoyi rose from his knees in excitement and ran to his mother's side.

"You leave tomorrow. Rest tonight," Oba Bode addressed the Owura men. "My servants will set you up with whatever you like." Oba Bode dismissed everyone from the room to sit alone and study his new expansion plans.

~

Ade and Amoyi were prepared to leave with the men the next morning. A carriage waited to carry them along with two horses for the Owura men.

Oba Bode approached them before they left. "You! Wa," he pointed to the spokesperson. The man smiled as he approached. His smile faded when he saw a machete handed to the oba. "Kneel," Oba Bode commanded the man.

As Bode raised the machete, Ade covered Amoyi's eyes. A servant stood nearby holding a wooden box. Another servant chased the spokesperson head and grabbed it by it's hair, blood rained as he carried it and placed it inside the box.

"That's a gift for your obi," Bode said as the servant handed one of the Owura messengers the box. "If I am ever dissatisfied, that's the fate of your people." Oba Bode turned to leave.

The men looked on, hiding the horror in their eyes. They didn't expect such an atrocity to be committed against them. They were simply messengers who agreed to help their friends, Tose and Sakin. They questioned what Sakin had in store for their village as they traveled back home with bad news and a beautiful woman.

Arundinlogbon

The sun began to paint the sky with splendid hues of pink and orange. The pink turned purple over time and the purple turned indigo until the sky was black with twinkling eyes. Drums signaled the messengers' return.

Sakin planned a feast for his reunion with Ade. Roasted hogs, yams and vegetables were placed on the table. Grapes, berries and other fruits were picked and placed in blue ceramic bowls. Sweet porridge made of honey and red berries mixed with mashed plantains complimented the night air. Chicken stewed with herbal leaves made it a tasteful treat.

A long mat laid in the Balogun's courtyard. He filled his old room with fresh flowers along the walls and rose petals on the bed. He looked regal in the green and yellow pattern garb Morayo sewed for him. Outfits were made for Morayo and Kisi in the same pattern. Although he was proud of his wife, he didn't want to push Ade away because he still loved her.

Ade arrived at the Balogun's compound by horse. An ęso helped her down. Tose, his wives and Kisi waited to meet her.

"I present to you Ayaba Ade," the ęso said as he walked with her hand in hand towards Tose.

"I've heard much about you," Tose said as he bowed his head with a smile.

"So, you're the beautiful woman from baba's stories. But, I don't remember you being a queen," Kisi said as she studied Ade.

Ade gently rested her palm on Kisi's head and she smiled. Amoyi peeked from behind her.

"Who's that?" Kisi asked.

"This is my son, Arèmo Amoyi," Ade announced as she put her hand on his shoulder to guide him to the front.

"We've prepared a feast for you," Tose said.

"While everything you've done is fitting, I don't come to you in good spirits. I fear for you and your people," Ade said.

Tose observed her sullen voice and frowned.

"You see, you wish to deal with a monster."

The messengers who fetched her hesitantly passed Tose the box covered in dried blood. "We must speak with him immediately. The situation has been strained," one of the messengers said.

Tose bent over to whisper to Kisi, "Tell your baba they're back. He'll know where to find us."

"Do you want to see my home?" Kisi asked Amoyi who nodded then ran off with her.

"Please, you must be tired. Let my wife show you where you'll be staying and care for you."

"Adupe." Ade followed one of his wives across the compound.

Kisi ran to her home with Amoyi. She passed her old house guarded by the Egungun. Amoyi stopped and gasped at the figure. When Kisi noticed Amoyi wasn't by her side she went back to him and grabbed his sweaty hand.

"Don't be afraid. That's my father. He's there to

make sure nothing bad happens to me," she said as they slowly walked passed the Egungun.

Kisi burst through the door. "She's here, baba." Kisi jumped into Sakin's lap. Morayo was fixing a basket of oils, cloths and jewelry. They were discussing what Ade meant to Sakin and why this meeting was important.

"Tani o?" Sakin asked as Amoyi came in behind Kisi. "Who's this?"

"This is Arèmo Amoyi." Kisi stood up proudly like the man introducing Ade. "Baba, grandfather wants to meet with you. It didn't seem nice. He was handed a bloody box."

Sakin and Morayo looked at each other. Concern flooded his eyes. "Children, do you want some sweet water?" Morayo asked.

"My mom makes the best sweet water," Kisi told Amoyi as she grabbed his hand. They waited patiently as they sat on the floor while Sakin slipped out the door.

He walked to the fire to meet Tose and the other men. He sat down with his back turned towards the Jefe guards. Tose pushed the box over, the earth crawled before it.

Sakin opened the box and saw the head of his spokesman riddled with maggot larvae moving about on his decaying skin.

"He said if he's not satisfied, this is what he will do to our people." The messenger paused to think about how he was going to tell his friend's family.

"We were friendly and he threaten us with war," the other messengers said.

Sakin closed the box and scratched his chin.

"Why does the oba do this?" Tose asked.

"He's a tyrant. He sees no man as a friendly." Sakin scratched the short, black beard on his chin. "But, I thought we had more time," Sakin said.

"What do you mean?" Tose asked.

"He sent Ade with guards to scout our village." Sakin nodded his head to one of the guardsmen studying the Egungun at the compound entrance. "This means he's looking to take this village by the next full moon," Sakin explained.

"How do you know this?" Tose asked.

"That's what my great-grandfather did."

"You speak as if he was a man of great importance," Tose said.

"Bẹẹni, my great-grandfather is Oba Akinbode Adesine. My brother was named after him."

The men's mouths dropped as they came to the conclusion about the man they've trusted for all these years.

"I am Omoba Sakin Adesine of Jefe. My brother is Oba Bode Adesine. That's the man I've been running from. That's the man I plan to overthrow." He paused to study the men's faces. "If you don't want to fight by my side I understand."

"Sakin, I already know who you are," Tose said. The fire flickered on his face. "Osun told me you would come. My granddaughter confirmed it many moons ago when she told my your stories. You've brought my family so much wealth. Put my wives' hearts at ease.

You saved my life. I'll fight with you this world and the next." He held out his hand.

Sakin nodded as he shook Tose's hand with both of his hands.

Ogunmefa

Affection from the woman he loved waited for him behind a door after seven long years. Even after he married Morayo he dreamt of this moment. Guards left the door unattended. He stood still outside the door. Hesitation almost buried the excitement while ideas of rejection and anger toyed with his mind. He took a deep breath and knocked.

"You may enter." He melted at the sound of her voice. His knees grew weak as he entered. Ade was pouring herself a cup of palm wine.

"May I have some?" Sakin asked as he closed the door.

Ade lifted her head at the sound of his voice. She turned and knocked the cup onto the floor. "Sakin?"

"Bẹẹni, it's me elẹwa." He smiled at her. He briskly walked to retrieve some cloths to place over the spilled wine. He grabbed the jug from her trembling hands and placed it on the table with the cup. He stood up and placed his arms around her. "I've dreamt of this moment many times. I didn't think you'd have me cleaning up palm wine," Sakin joked.

He pulled her shoulder back to study her face. He grazed his thumb from her cheekbone to her neck where he found a scar. "Oh, elęwa. What has he done to you?" He could see the youthful woman he fell in love with had became callous in her eyes and stern in her jaw. Her golden aura had grown faint. It rejuvenated every second within his arms.

"For so long I thought you were dead," she cried. "I prayed you weren't and that you'd return to me. The Gods and Goddesses finally smile upon me," she smiled.

Sakin engaged her lips. He remembered their warm, softness. He could taste the salt of her tears. They stayed in the embrace for a moment. They separated and he wiped her tears. He took her hand and sat her down on the bed.

"I didn't mean to betray our love, Sakin," she

spoke. Her eyes grew sad. "I had to marry Bode to protect my people."

Sakin flared inside. "I understand, Ade." He
figured that much would happen in his absence. "You
didn't betray me."

"He cut my father's hand off to force my hand
and threatened to sell my people as slaves to the yuvo,"
she explained further. With each statement her face
soften and her shoulders dropped. She felt the weight
of seven years melt away. "He took my people for slaves
anyway."

"When did this happen?"

"No more than two weeks ago." Ade dropped her
eyes. "Our son witnessed it all."

The anger thawed when he heard of a child he
fathered with her. It took him back to the evening they
made love.

"Amoyi?" he asked with a smile, thinking of the
boy he just met.

"You've already met him."

"Bẹẹni, my daughter brought him to our home."

Ade's smile dimmed.

"She's my iyawo's daughter. Her father was killed in battle."

"Your wife?" She looked a bit skeptical but not surprised since so much time was stolen from them.

"Bẹẹni, her name is Morayo. She's a wonderful woman. She nursed me to health when I arrived at this village. Her father-in-law gave me a home allowing me to recover."

"How did you get here?"

"I sank to the bottom of the river where I met a woman that was half fish. She took me to some mystical place underwater. I thought it was you because she sang the same song you sang to me when we were together."

"You met Osun." Ade smiled with tears forming again in her eyes.

"Bẹẹni, Osun." Sakin paused to thank the Goddess. "She started the healing process so I wouldn't loose so much blood. Next thing I know, I met Tose Balogun at the base of a tall waterfall. A fall I shouldn't have survived."

Ade rubbed his face. He kissed her hand. "I'm happy your still alive. I told Amoyi stories about you. He doesn't know you're his father though. I feared Bode would find out and attempt to take his life."

"You've done well, Ade." He kissed her forehead.

They were disturbed by a knock on the door. He heard Kisi laughing behind it. Morayo entered with the children and a beautiful basket on her head. Sakin got up and met her at the door. He kissed her cheek. He held her hand and grabbed Kisi's hand as well. Amoyi walked over to his mother.

"Ade, iyawo mi o Morayo pelu omo mi Kisi."

Ade rose and walked towards Morayo. "I'm please to meet you." She bowed her head slightly.

Morayo removed the basket from her head and handed it to Ade. "This is for you."

Ade took it and place it on the table next to the jug of wine. "Adupe." She walked over to hug Morayo. "For taking care of Sakin all these years. Just to know he's alive makes the world easier to bear," she said in

Morayo's ear.

"Can we go eat now? I'm starving." Kisi interrupted then ran out the door.

They laughed. Ade grabbed Morayo's hand and walked out the door with her. "You know you remind me of my sister," she said. "She knows how to prepare oils too. You'd love her."

Sakin smiled as they walked off talking. He placed his hand on Amoyi's shoulder. "Your mother is a fine queen." I know you will be a fine oba one day." Amoyi smiled at the compliment. He was accustomed to hearing otherwise from Oba Bode.

"Is it true you wrestled a leopard with your bear hands?" Amoyi's eyes lit up.

"Not entirely. I had a spear too," Sakin chuckled. "One day, you will too," he said as they walked out the hut.

Amoyi enjoyed the feast as musicians played. He ran around with the other children playing games until the moon was high in the sky. Laughter sprang from his mother, a sound he rarely heard, as she accepted her hosts like she accepted his aunts. Many villagers came to greet him and his mom with gifts. Some of them stayed for the celebration, to enjoy food and drinks. He watched as Sakin danced in the air, rolling and flipping like a leaf. He practiced some of the moves with him. He enjoyed it even more when Sakin explained they were some of the moves he used on the leopard and the praised Doye.

Later that night, full with savory food and exhausted from the festivities, the children were sent off to bed. The guards were placed in separate chambers, eased by drunkenness and women. They took advantage since they didn't get to enjoy themselves often.

Sakin invited Ade and Doye to his hut where they met with Tose and Morayo to begin their plans. Ade informed Sakin of Oba Bode's antics of village take overs. She described how he raided her home with horsemen and guns. They decided the best place to meet Oba Bode was in Jefe where he felt the safest.

"You'll tell him we're conquerable. He'll lead his men south along the river. While within the igbo we'll attack him from all sides. I'll meet him with Tose from the west." Sakin drew a map.

"I'm strong but I can't withstand ibons. And we don't have enough men to take a faction this big," Doye spoke.

"Doye's right. That's the problem Owura suffered with every war," Tose agreed.

The room fell silent as Sakin thought.

"I know how to get more men. Bode does business with the yuvo along the big water in the west. He raids a city and sells the captives to several of those men. Many of them have ibons they trade with."

Sakin rubbed his forehead. It was a viable way to overthrow his brother. There would be various type of villages who specialized in different weaponry and magic.

"We'll free them," Sakin spoke sternly. "We'll use the fishermen boat to bring the young and old to a place we set up near here. Morayo I need you there to take care of them."

Morayo nodded with fear in her eyes. She hated

talks of war since that's how she lost her first husband. She wondered if Sakin would be successful at all. It was too early to give him up, especially since she recently found out she was pregnant. Sakin squeezed her hand as if he heard her thoughts.

"I will not fight with a bunch of people who couldn't protect their own village." Doye shook his head.

"Don't worry. I know how to make them stronger. I just need to see Baba Oju." Sakin looked at Doye. "They'll fight again. And this time." He paused as he stood up. "They will not lose."

Ogunmeje

Ade made her journey back to Jefe while Sakin
led all the men, fitted for war, to the village of Koso,
where the temple of Sango dwelled and his mentor Oju
lived with his students. The trip was hard for his men
since the season grew wet and the nights were cold.
Mud splattered up their legs as they walked in the rain.
At night, they gathered around a large fire.

On one occasion the fire attracted hunters who
questioned them about their intentions since the large
quantity of men could perform a small invasion. Sakin
assured them they weren't seeking to invade them only
Jefe. Satisfied with Sakin's explanations the hunters
agreed to help since they heard about the evil king that
would one day invade their home and sell their people
as slaves. Sakin and his men were given food and horses for their quest. In return, Sakin gave them bags of
cowries. That repeated in other villages along his jour-

ney to Koso.

At Koso, the men were spotted by a drummer as they approached through the igbo. One drummer within the forest alerted the drummers at the Koso entrance. The drums were closer and closer until Sakin emerged from the thick foliage with his men and walked across the plains.

The drummers were furious because the troop of men resembled an army rather than a band of travelers. Sakin stopped in the middle of the plains. He saw the men with swords and tall shields make a wall between him and the village. He called for his drummer to tell them they were friendly. The Koso warriors sent a representative to speak with them once they heard the message.

"Tani se?" the man asked as he approached.

"I'm Omoba Sakin Adesine."

"You lie. Omoba Sakin is long dead."

"I've reemerged."

"Impossible!"

"Nothing is impossible when you serve Sango."

The tall man with a thick beard and tightly coiled hair studied Sakin and the men behind him.

"If you don't believe me take me to Baba Oju. I'll leave my weapons here along with my men."

Feeling unthreatened by one man, the representative agreed and had Sakin follow him while Sakin's men rested in the plains.

A tall, fat rock figure with conches for eyes and a mouth sat at the entrance of the village covered in offerings. The shrine represented Elegba, the God of communication that governs all crossroads. Sakin stopped to greet the shrine by touching his forefingers to the earth. He then reached into his traveling sack and presented a pouch of cowries.

Behind the wall of men were people enjoying life. Children kicked a woven ball around. Women performed their chores with their daughters doing the same nearby. The men congregated around tables playing games of ayo as they talked about village and familial affairs. It was how Sakin remembered it. There were some familiar faces- aged, but there were also many new faces since the village had grown.

The temple of Sango sat in the middle of the village. The sun hovered directly above it. History said Sango was once upset his worshippers because they broke a taboo. They were performing witchcraft against each other. Sango set the temple afire by a single lightning bolt. Some people were trapped inside. The people didn't know what to do. Every time they splashed water on the flames the fire flared pushing them back. The people begged for Sango to free the ones inside and spare the village from the flames. The fire spread. The people panicked.

One little girl sang to Sango with all her heart while praying for the people inside. She walked into the burning building from the plains with a bitter kola nut in her hands. They saw the fire part for her as she walked all the way to the temple. The little girl walked inside the temple and knelt before the shrine. She offered the bitter kola nut to the shrine. Not long after the flames vanished leaving a blackened building.

The little girl was Oju's grandmother fifteen generations back. She left the family in charge of the temple worship ever since. Fire still spontaneously occurs within and outside the building. When it does every one stops what their doing to touch their foreheads to the earth and recite a prayer:

Egun ara oyo

Ara ewo ara ede

Omo odo oba

Ti ó ba nse

Won a ma a sóre' kiri

Won a ní ịtale ló nja wón

Oníle ori okè fiti

Isale ká mi mo

Ti wón ba pe Oya

Ko dáhún ni ile irá

Ti wón ba pe ori

Sakin met Oju outside the temple.

"This man says he's Omoba Sakin Adesine. But, that man's dead," the escorter said as he and Sakin stood before Oju.

"Bééni. But, as Obalube lives so does Sakin." Oju laughed as he grabbed Sakin for an embrace. "I've prayed for this moment," he said as they parted.

"You didn't believe I was dead?"

"Not at all. I did too many sacrifices to ensure your well being," he laughed. "To believe you were dead would be to believe Sango is not king." Sakin laughed with him. "Besides, Ifa told me you'd return someday. I already know what I have to do."

Sakin told Oju about his men waiting in the plains. Oju ordered the guard to let the men into the village. Sakin asked the man to bring Tose and Doye to him. The guard did as instructed and Sakin introduced his comrades to Oju.

Oju laughed as he shook Tose's hand. "You're the man I've seen before when I was traveling. Wow, Sakin's the man you were suppose to help."

Tose looked at Oju's face until he remembered. "Bééni, I've seen you before. It's true."

"And you'll reap the benefits the rest of your life and so will your children."

Sakin thought about the fortune he planned for Tose the moment he allowed him to stay in his compound. More land for him and his sons to rule along with the prestigious title of 'hand of the king.'

The men followed Oju to his large compound. They were swarmed and taken care of by women who were all Oju's wives and daughters. Doye was struck by a young woman who was as beautiful as the midnight sky. Oju noticed the attraction between the two.

"You want my daughter?" Oju asked Doye as the men enjoyed themselves with food and drink.

"Bééni." Doye nodded.

"She's yours," Oju said. "She'll calm you down and maybe your face can keep some sort of decency."

Tose and Sakin laughed.

"You'll endow me when Sakin rewards you. I already accept. And you and her will give me big, strong grandsons."

Doye sipped his wine. "You speak as if you know the future." He wondered how Oju could see his intentions.

"I don't know the future. But, I see enough of it," Oju laughed.

After an evening of merriment Oju took Sakin to his divining ile where they sat and smoked. Sakin explained his life after plunging into the river. They recounted the past and how Sakin utilized some ritual practices in order to defeat Doye and bring Tose's sons back to him through Egungun.

"You want to know how to defeat Bode." Tose struck the heart of Sakin's visit. Sakin nodded.

Oju grabbed his turtle shell opele while he recited prayers to the Gods. He touched the opele to Sakin's forehead before touching it to the earth once and on the mat three times. He let the opele dance in the air, the shells rotated on the chain, before he casted on the mat. He smiled as he interpreted the signs.

Oju spoke. "You've pleased your Ancestors and the ones of many others. They'll fight with you." He watched Sakin nod with understanding. "You've already fulfilled offerings to Legba and Egungun." Oju paused as he listened to the odus. "There are two more things you must do before you leave."

The next day, Sakin went to the market to find a male goat and a black pig. He gathered all his men together that afternoon. His numbers grew as the warriors of Koso agreed to join the legendary omoba in battle. They provided him with more weapons and a multitude of shields with a red background and white axes painted on them. Oju's students went around outfitting every man for war giving them something red to drink and some meat to eat.

It was beginning to rain when Sakin, Tose and Doye sat with Oju inside the temple. They each offered their own sacrifices. The black pig was sacrificed first. Oju's students took the carcass to strip its skin to collect its bones. Afterwards they mixed the bones, they powdered down with a mortar and pestle, with droplets of blood and herb infused water inside a jug. The corked jug was handed to Tose.

"Every man, woman and child you free along the coast must sip this," Oju said as he handed Tose the jug. "Every man willing to fight must receive their weapon from you," he told Doye.

Oju walked to his monument to Sango and grabbed one ax and another from the shrine built for Sakin when he was a boy. He placed them on the earth in the middle of the room. He walked the goat over to the axes while reciting a prayer. He took the knife from his waist strap and pointed it to the sky. He dipped it in water and sprinkled water on the goat's head and hoofs. He thanked the goat for its sacrifice before he slit its throat. The blood squirted onto the axes. Oju and a student lifted the goat over Sakin's head while he relished in the memorable warmth. They then laid the goat next to the axes to let the blood flow around them. Oju walked to Sakin who was covered in eje and told Sakin to stick out his tongue. He wiped the blade on Sakin's tongue.

When the ritual was finished Oju asked everyone to leave. "You must rest here," Oju turned to tell Sakin as he walked out with the others.

Sakin watched the flies swarm the congealing blood. As he watched the flies he heard thunderous knocking before the creak of the door. He turned when he heard the door shut. There was no one there. Instead, he found himself in the middle of a circle of trees. He looked around and saw deers walking. He heard birds chirping and gliding. He watched all of the forest creatures go about their business.

The animals fled as gray clouds encapsulated the sun. Rain drops pounded the ground like stampedes of wilder beast shaking Sakin. Sakin tried to balance himself by staying low to the ground with outstretched arms. Out of the clouds came a striking, golden jagged rod. It penetrated the earth by his feet. It stayed. The sky invitingly rumbled. Sakin grabbed the lightning rod and saw the earth disappear, replaced by white fluffiness as electricity surged through him. He looked up and saw nothing but white space appear. He let go of the rod and stood on smoky pillows

In the vast whiteness surrounding him, he heard tumultuous footsteps. Sakin's shadow grew from behind and walked towards a shimmering stone, each step shuddering the heavens of earth. Sakin felt power climb his legs as he walked behind the giant being. The shimmering stone transformed into a giant aafin as they came near. Rubies, laid in swirling patterns, flickered like flames. The aafin grew larger than the figure now distinguished as a man wearing red and white cloth with bolts of lightning patterned throughout wrapped around his waist. He carried a large double headed ax in his left hand dripping droplets of blood morphing into a walkway of rose petals to the aafin. Long golden stairs led to the aafin where two thrones sat in between spiral columns and an atrium with a fire pit in the middle.

A wind dissipated the whiteness above. Sakin watched a tornado emerge as tall as the male being. The tornado transfigured into a shapely woman's body with reddish black skin whose hair curled and wavered in the air. Her dress ended in whorls of fire. The woman, Oya, walked beside her husband.

Sakin looked above at the midnight sky twinkling like eyes. Colossal firestones flew pass him. Comets clashed into each other generating driblets of rain penetrating the cloud floor, striking the earth.

The village people were dismayed as it rained. The strikes of lightning they saw set the temple ablaze. All of them prostrated while the men unfamiliar with the history frantically ran around searching for water to calm the flames in order to retrieve their leader.

Oju smiled at the extravaganza.

"We have to get Sakin out!" Tose shouted over the disarray to Oju.

"Go ahead, but I'm not fireproof," Oju laughed.

"How can you laugh about such a thing? He may already be dead." Tose tried to reason with someone he now thought to be a mad man.

"Either way he's with Sango. Neither you nor I can take him back now." Oju sat down and watched the flames dance.

"What do we do now?" Doye asked as he looked at Tose.

"Just watch," Oju responded.

The being Sakin knew as Sango reached the gigantic aafin, turned around to sit on his throne. He was joined by the tornado woman, his queen Oya. Sango wore a crown of cowries. His eyes were black as coal. Unaware of what else to do Sakin prostrated.

"You may rise," Sango spoke with a resounding voice.

Out of respect Sakin continued to kneel before him and waited for the God to speak again. Sango gave Sakin jewels to aid his quest and what he must do. When finished Sango asked Sakin if there was something he wanted to know.

"How did my father die?" Sakin wondered ever since the guard announced his father's death on the hill.

"Suffocated by the hatred of his son."

Sakin's heart sank in grief of the truth. That grief turned into anger. He pondered on any other questions.

"Will I avenge my father's death and the atrocities my brother has committed?"

Sango looked at him with pearly black eyes. "You will see soon enough," he paused then smiled. "Dance for me."

Sakin heard a band of unseen drummers. He rose. He felt heavier. A red and white beaded vest and red cloth around his waist dressed him. Blood covered axes sat firmly in his hands.

As he danced blood rained from the axes. Jaw muscles protruded as he clenched his teeth. His nostrils flared and his eyes burned. He pumped his hips back and forth. He leaped in the air and spun around. He spat fire from his mouth as he exhaled.

The doors flung open. People watched in awe as Sakin emerged from the temple. His hips and feet spun like a winged seed spinning in the air. As he walked, the ground shook. The further he was from the temple the more the flames dwindled. The people stayed out of arm's length and watched heat rise off Sakin's body.

All the warriors who waited rose as Sakin walked towards them. Sakin went to Doye and pounded his bare chest, the axes marking an x across it in blood. To everyone it looked like a boulder pounding against another boulder. Doye's big nostrils flared.

Tose responded the same when Sakin pounded his chest. The three of them struck all the warriors. Villages near and far heard the reverberating sound, stopped what they were doing and paid homage to the Thunder God, Sango.

Sakin marched. The warriors followed. Oju smiled and shouted, "Kawo Kabiesi!" The villagers repeated, "Hail the King!"

The warriors cut days into hours as they ran swiftly across the plains and through the igbo.

Mejidinlogbon

Sakin smelled the salt in the air. He knew he was near the coast. He raised his fist signaling the men to halt. He let them rest as he climbed a tree to scope the area. He saw two large ships in the water. Small camps of men lounged around small fires. Large numbers of captives were held in small cages. People walked around on the ships performing morning chores.

After his feet touched the earth he told Doye and Tose his plan. He had the Koso men follow Doye. He ordered the Owura men to follow Tose. Sakin ordered his drummer to let the captives know their presence.

"You hear that?" a yuvo asked the men around the fire.

"Man, you're just hearing thunder. It's been doing that for hours now."

"Ssshhh," the man raised his thin fingers to his pink lips. "No, I hear drums."

The men on the beach listened and were startled when they realized they too heard drums. They looked at each other confused. No savage had ever attacked them along the shores, most of them had agreements with nearby kingdoms. They all got up to wait in line for a gun.

The black sky turned orange. The men marveled at that sight until they realized they were fiery spears covering the sky. They scattered out of range. The spears impaled some of them from the back, from the chest or through the neck. Barrels of alcohol exploded. Crates of gun powder erupted sending chards of wood everywhere. Caged captives rattled the timber erected in the sand, weakening their enclosure.

A smoky haze ascended from the burning spears. Warriors shouted as they emerged from the forest. The yuvo fired their guns. Disappointment with its failure to slow the warriors down and fear resonated in their faces as they reloaded their weapons. A few warriors opened the cages and shattered the captive's chains. A group of them led the women and children back to the forest. The men were given shields, spears, machetes, bows and arrows with a small concoction to drink.

Sakin and Doye led warriors through the water to the boat with their shields and weapons bound to their backs. Sakin went to one ship and Doye went to another. The sound of their knives picking the sides of the vessel as they climbed were drowned by the battle on the shore. The warriors climbed like spiders until they reached the top. Aboard they were greeted by open fire. In the midst of sailors reloading their guns the warriors stabbed them in the chest, cut their throats and impaled their stomachs.

A nude obsidian black woman fled the captains quarters screaming. She got on her hands and knees to crawl out of harm's way. A knife on the deck fed her thirst for revenge. The old, hairy captain tried to fasten his pants as he scurried from the captain's quarters. The knife dug into his heart when he came out of the room. Blood slowly dyed his white shirt as he traced the black arm to the face of the fierce woman.

Sakin noticed the woman as he fought. "Ibi ti o wa awon iyoku ti o?" he asked. "Where are the rest of you?"

"Si isale nibe." The man covered in the enemy's blood frightened her yet she felt freed from hell. "Down there." She pointed below.

"Laaye won," Sakin bellowed as he cut the neck of a man running towards him. "Free them."

She ran into the captain's quarters in search of the keys. Once she found them she ran around the corner to the black iron gate. She jiggled a key into the lock the way she watched the men do during the day until she found the magical one. She heard a loud click and the squeaking gate as it opened.

All the captives below looked to see who was coming. By the sounds of everything upstairs their prayers were answered. The woman ran down the stairs. She stopped at the end of the aisle and tried each key until everyone was freed. They all ran upstairs. They kicked and spat on the yuvo's dead bodies.

Sakin examined the people. Many of them were

in good condition. The men were big and strong. He could tell some of them were warriors in their home village. They spanned from young to old.

"Some of you were just in a bad place at a bad time," he paused. "Others are from villages raided by my brother Oba Bode Adesine. I, Omoba Sakin Adesine set you free. If you want your revenge fight with me and this is what I will give you."

They watched patches of the shore burn. They saw people along the woods singing and dancing, calling them back to the shore.

Sakin had all the women, children and elders transported to the shore on the small boats attached to the side of the ships. Many men swam back to the shore. When they were all one, Sakin set up camps to provide them with rest and meals. Lines formed to talk to him about where their loved ones were and what happened to their villages. He couldn't answer any of their questions.

Women offered themselves to him as a wife, servant or concubine. He declined many of their requests explaining there were plenty of his warriors in need of a wife. He said that to all except Fasina, the first woman he met on the ship. He noted her beauty and veracity. He kept her close with tasks to accomplish.

Mules hauled women, children, elders and the sick away to Owura where Morayo cared for them while he planned the next attack. He sent the ships along a river to store them in case of need.

Scouts returned with news of another party of yuvos a day away up the coast with more ships and captives. A camp was set up near the target so food and medicine would be close for the newly freed people.

They struck the camp in the night letting many of their warriors quench their thirst of revenge. Sakin was disappointed the encampment didn't have the Jembe people. So he continued the search until he found them.

After his successful campaigns he wondered about the people he couldn't free, about the people already making their way to the new world. He prayed that Ade's people weren't among them. He apologized to her spirit and everybody's Ancestors he couldn't make it to the taken ones in time.

Sakin didn't know this wasn't a new occurrence, people were stolen and taken to the new world for over seven decades. Since Jefe was much further inland he decided to make it a safe haven and vowed to have men along the perimeter to watch out for slave catchers and their ships. If he heard about one he'd burn it to the bottom of the beautiful sea with their captors still on it. Any oba selling people into captivity like his brother he would destroy.

Mokandilogbon

Essien arrived at the aafin flushed with enclosed anger. Calmly he approached the oba before visiting his compound to let his wife know her beloved son was murdered. He hoped he could ease her pain with the thought of avenging their son's death. He, essentially a messenger, couldn't do that alone. He needed to rally the king.

"I humbly come before you seeking a mutual agreement. The Jama have taken your sister for a slave, raped her, striped her of her children. On top of that they murdered my son." Essien motioned for his servant to show his son's head in the box. "They wanted to let you know 'the war was never over'. In the meantime, your sister was sold to the yuvo to be taken to the new world."

Oba Bode flicked his cigar ashes into a ashtray on his table. He pulled from the cigar again while he looked at Essien. He released the smoke then shrugged his shoulders. "What do you expect me to do?"

Essien was baffled by this question. It was clear in his mind and any other man's mind on what to do. Even if he didn't care about his family, the threat to his pride should've been enough.

"My oba they've let you know they only want to fight. With the resources you've gained from trading with the yuvo success is a surety."

"I have debts I still have to pay."

"If it's debts your worried about I will pay."

"You'd be willing to sacrifice your family? Because that's what I need, bodies."

Essien's jaw tightened. He was tired. Before him he saw a boy that thought he was a man because he killed people. A boy in a man's body still riddled with jealousy of a dead brother. A boy who was completely unaware of how to guide a people let alone himself.

"I'm assuming your answer is a no. Go home Essien. Go home and bury your son." Oba Bode pulled from his cigar again.

Essien left. He went home with the girl he found
on his way home in a Jama village and his son's body.
He told his wife about everything even about the
grandchild he still had to find. He watched her weep.
After his son's funeral he rode north-west. There was
still someone who could defeat Bode. A queen who refused to succumb to the enemy taking her people with
smiling faces.

When he arrived she was away in battle. He
stayed a few days waiting for her return. Once she returned they met.

"Ayaba Niyah. I've heard much about you during
my travels. I've heard how you tirelessly fight the yuvo
and return our people back to their homes. I'm apart
of a kingdom with a treacherous king that has broken a
taboo," Essien explained as he stood before the younger
woman.

"Many kings have done so," she retorted. "Every
time I fight the yuvo they find a brother of mines willing to wage war with me. And for what? Money? Land?
What makes your king different?"

"The difference my queen is there's a woman, the queen, who'd be willing to align herself with your cause since it's one we all believe in. With him defeated she'll be put into power with a whole army at your disposal. A very large one at best."

Ayaba Niyah chuckled. "Not if I destroy them to kill him."

Essien studied her strong body. She was tall, muscularly thin, yet still had the femininity of a woman. She was very attractive and didn't have time for the antics of his broken heart.

"What if you could do so discreetly? Then you wouldn't lose so much of your army trying to gain one."

She nonchalantly shrugged her shoulders. "Every so called king I fight returns home licking his wounds, upset that he was beaten by a woman. The yuvo then supplies him with more resources to fight me. I've free thousands of people," she paused to drink water. "I will help you."

Essien prepared himself to thank her but stopped when she raised her hand and shook her head.

"I will help you because I've heard about your king and I despise him," Ayaba Niyah continued. "And because you've asked me. You don't have to thank me for doing something we're all supposed to be doing- protecting our people, our land and destroying anyone who tries to break our ties to our Ancestors."

Essien smiled at the fiery woman. "I will let you eat your meal in peace." Essien turned to leave.

"Please, join me olori Essien." She waved at a seat across from her modest table. "We have much to talk about."

Ogbon

Word spread throughout the nearby villages of the warriors along the coast freeing captives before they sailed into the blue abyss. These men were called Eje Okunrin, the Blood Men. Traders gave their portrayals of what happened, taking the stories from the old freed men making their way to Owura.

The frightened yuvo were told how the late evening sky turned bright and the Eje Okunrin were impervious to bullets. Most of the captains tried to set sail early. Their captives were becoming unruly animals when they heard the stories too and they didn't want to lose their black gold cargo. For many of the ships, it was too late. They were raided just as their ships tried to sail off. Oba Bode heard these stories and agreed to send a militia to protect his business partner.

When Oba Bode wasn't thinking about the Eje Okunrin he was happy. Amoyi was thrilled to train when he returned to Jefe and Oba Bode was excited about his son's new interest. As he trained with Amoyi he found himself on his back as Amoyi had a clever combative flying style.

Life appeared to be better since Ade and Amoyi returned. Oba Bode was close enough to smell the sweet scent of Ade many occasions. When she offered herself to him he was surprised, but he found himself disinterested because there was new word about the Eje Okunrin. He prodded for people to find out who led them. He thought it would be an admirable foe since every village he took was too easy for true enjoyment.

Oba Bode wanted to take Owura, but his plans were out of focus since the raids on the coast. Ade even told him the best time to strike. Before he attacked, he needed to make sure there was somewhere to sell the captives and their gold.

With every success of the Eje Okunrin, Ade retreated to her room to rejoice. The only thing leaving her discontent was the lack of news about her people. Sakin promised to find them which was the only reason she figured he hadn't attacked Jefe yet. So after a brief rejoice she prayed for Sakin's well being and the return of her people.

When Ade heard Essien's reports of Adunni, she prayed Sakin found his sister. By the time Ade returned, she missed Ode's funeral and Essien. Essien's wife accepted her condolences and gave her Adunni's daughter, Abioye, who Ade kept from Bode.

Late at night, Bode complained to Mofeyisade. She laid seductively in the bed, waiting for him. She listened to his plight and commented when she felt necessary. She wondered if he noticed her growing belly. He never seemed to. She took pride in what she carried for him. She knew he didn't love her, at least that's what she thought. To her it was the insurance of his survival, to make sure he had a portal through which he could return. She would raise the child to be like his father since the baby she carried was Oba Bode's true offspring.

One of the late evenings spent with Oba Bode, Mofeyisade closed the door of his room to get more palm wine. She stumbled across Ade whispering with Essien downstairs in front of the garden. Mofeyisade never liked the two. She felt Bode's life was in danger whenever they were around. She had heard about the attempts Ade made on Bode's life. She wanted to retaliate. However, when she saw Ade hiding scars the next few days, she smiled to herself.

"… Eje Okunrin?" Essien questioned. He remained quiet when he saw the servant walk pass.

Mofeyisade watched the floor as she walked to the kitchen to reach the wine cellar. She stayed behind the door of the kitchen to listen further.

"Tell your aunt I would love to meet her after the celebration."

"Will do," Essien said as he bowed and turned to leave.

Mofeyisade was startled when she saw Ade walking towards the kitchen. It was nowhere to hide so she opened the door as if she were leaving.

"Ayaba Ade. I'm sure you have someone to fetch your needs. Tocarra should be available. If not I'll wake her."

"No need. Some times I like to do things myself." Ade studied the woman with a smile. She knew Mofeyisade was in love with Bode. How?, was something she couldn't imagine. When she looked at the baby blooming in Mofeyisade's stomach, she couldn't ignore it anymore. It wasn't the child she was concerned about though. The child would come into the world innocent. She was worried about what its mother would teach them. "I see you're further along."

"Bẹẹni."

"And the father. Is he excited?"

"I don't know. He's been busy taking care of his chores."

"I see." Ade chuckled. "Well, anyhow. Run along. Oba Bode doesn't like to be kept waiting."

Mofeyisade scurried off back to Oba Bode's room. When she got there he was asleep. She knew waking him made him physically violent. So, she fell asleep waiting to tell him about the eery feeling. When she woke up he was already gone.

Mokanlelogbon

A scout returned with more news of another encampment. Sakin feared they were veering too far off course from Jefe. So, he told the men this would be their last raid until he overthrew his brother. Their number multiplied to a suitable number to complete the task comfortably. If not a sneak attack was still in his favor. It wasn't bad that he had ships to ride the waves of the rivers too.

Owura increased so much that Morayo had to send people to Koso and other villages along the way. The freed people didn't mind since they were given gold to start a new life in the villages.

Again Sakin struck at night. Sakin waited with his militia by a bank where the river connected with the sea. One by one a warrior stood in the crest where salt water turned fresh, recited a brief prayer for victory before they walked until submerged by the greenish-blue water. A myriad of men followed Doye to the ships. Another squad was sent with Tose across the river to strike from the forest.

Sakin had a peculiar feeling though. Everything seemed too quiet. He couldn't hear the yuvo singing and laughing like the former camps. Their fires were dim. He knew they were prepared to fight.

Tose ordered the men to strike. As the first group made it midway on the beach spears jutted from the ground penetrating them. Unaware of how far the men laid he sent another group, they were ensnared sooner. Tose ordered the men to regroup. Black warriors fell from the trees stabbing them in their backs.

The bull horn call alerted Sakin something went wrong with Tose and his men. He didn't hear any gun shots. He knew his men were being attacked by men of their type. He sent a few more men out to sea and swam with them. Sakin ordered a larger number of men to go back to the forest and strike the attackers from behind. He had another plan once he got out to the ships. He told them to go as deep into the forest as they could while fighting.

Doye wasted no time in getting onto the ships. The yuvo were busy cheering their allies on the beach. They didn't care Eje Okunrin were crawling up their boats. Doye told his men to keep quiet when they got onto the ships. Some spectators throats were cut. Doye noticed the yuvos had company. He and the others hesitated attacking the black men. The black men shot and speared them. He motioned for his men to slay everyone on deck.

One Eje Okunrin crumpled the gate open with his foot after several tries. He and another ran down the stairs and found yuvos waiting with ibons. He held his shield up in time and charged at the men who opened fire. He kicked them back and a captive wrapped chains around the yuvos' neck strangling them.

The warrior struck the chains with his machete several times until it broke. One of the first men freed lunged on the Eje Okunrin, punching and kicking him. Many of the people still taking off their shackles cheered on the Eje Okunrin. They yelled, "impostor," to let the man know they all were not like him. The Eje Okunrin subdued the man in a chokehold.

He looked at the captives, confused on who to trust.

"Brothers, sisters. If anyone tries to proclaim you a slave, kill them. Kill them with your bare hands if you have to. If you know the impostors break their necks for betraying their Ancestors," the Eje Okunrin said.

The freed men yelled as they left their shackles behind. The impostors' necks were broken while they pleaded for forgiveness. The freed men ran upstairs and grabbed anything to use as a weapon. Yuvos and their partners were struck over the heads with canon balls. Others used their bare hands to snap necks from behind.

When the sailors on the other ship saw what happened, they adjusted. They sent men all around the deck to see if any Eje Okunrin were coming. They found Sakin and his men jumping aboard by the time they acted. The ship was soon overran like the other.

Sakin noticed some of the black men aboard as men from Jefe's Army. A warrior charged at him. He ran up a pole to evade him, flung himself upside down and sheared his head off. When the freed captives ran aboard, Sakin's heart settled. He noticed some of the faces as Jembe. He found them.

Sakin found canons on the ships like the other ones. In one raid the yuvo used them. It didn't take long to figure out how it worked. There were two men on each, one loading and another setting it afire. Canons flew from the ships and pounded the beach as far as the forest. Spears and body fragments flew into the air with sand. The Eje Okunrin on the beach stayed out of range. They saw their attackers were distracted by the explosive boulders reaching the shore. The Eje Okunrin threw their spears, impaling them.

Some of the enemy tried to get away. They were cut off within the forest. Eje Okunrin came from trees slicing their heads, chests and legs. The Jefe Army could see nothing but death as they were attacked from all sides.

The Eje Okunrin persevered. Sakin and Doye took the first boat back to the the beach with some women and children. They carried barrels back to camp where food was prepared and healing supplies were rationed. Fasina led the women in providing the refreshments and deciding where people should go.

Sakin met with Tose and Doye after taking a look at all the freed people. Doye was already resting in a chair and eating food prepared for him by a woman who grew sweet on him. Tose stood behind a Jefe warrior with his spear to his back. The man's hands were bound behind him and his shoulder leaked blood.

"This man says he's with Jefe," Tose said as he pierced the man's wound with the spear.

"I noticed some of the warriors on the ship." Sakin placed his axes on a red cloth next to the ayo set and maps on the table. "Why did the oba send you?" He turned to the man.

"There's only one I have to answer to." The man spat at Sakin's feet.

Sakin walked from behind the table. "I am Omoba Sakin Adesine. The brother of your oba."

The man's eyes widen in disbelief. "It can't be. I saw you drown with my own eyes."

"Yet, here I am." Sakin grabbed Tose's spear. "You must be blind."

"What are you going to do with him?" Doye asked with a full mouth.

"I'm going to send him back. I want you to tell my brother I'm coming for his head."

"You won't survive against oba. He's a god." The man laughed.

"A yoo ri eyi ti oba ye ki o ti kuna." Sakin tipped over a carved leopard representing the king with the tip of the spear. "We shall see which king should fall."

Tose lifted the man to his feet. The man groaned from the handling of his shoulder and told him to run. The man ran out as Fasina walked in with a bowl of food beneath her exposed breast for Sakin and a gourd of palm wine. Other women walked in the same for Tose and Doye.

Fasina brushed her shoulder against Sakin's chest

while looking into his eyes as she walked by to place the bowl on the table. The men laughed at the interaction.

"My king. There's a woman who's insisted on meeting with you," Fasina said as she placed the bowl down.

"Let her in."

Sakin was astounded when he saw his younger sister standing before him with a small child. He jumped from his stool and ran over to Adunni and hugged her.

"Sister, what has happened to you?" he asked.

Adunni explained as Sakin held her in his arms. He promised once the kingdom was his he would avenge her honor. He had her set up near his sleeping mat. When he sat down he found his appetite had left.

"Is there anything else the king needs?" Fasina asked as she bowed her head.

Sakin looked up from his food. "There's one more thing."

Mejilelogbon

No one was more adept than Oba Bode at ayo until Amoyi came back from Owura. Amoyi's counting abilities subdued him every time. Oba Bode admired the boy's ability to outsmart him. That cleverness even became more apparent in combat sparring.

Ade hummed as she watched her son beat Oba Bode again. She daydreamed about Sakin overthrowing the monster she was forced to marry.

"What's that you're humming?" the annoyed oba asked.

"Something my mother used to sing to me," she replied pleasantly.

"Stop. It vexes me," he grunted.

"Oba!" the bloody warrior Sakin let go burst into the room.

"I tried to stop him, but he says he has urgent news about the coast," Tekun said as he hurried in behind the soldier.

The warrior held his bleeding shoulder, pale, drained of life.

"What is it?" Oba Bode rose.

"It's your brother. He's alive!"

Ade smiled. Oba Bode's tongue was momentarily paralyzed.

"What do you mean?" Tekun questioned.

"Omoba Sakin has risen from the land of the dead. He's the leader of the Eje Okunrin. He attacked the yuvo and released the Jembe. He's on his way here now," the warrior said as he panted.

Oba Bode sat down like he was winded.

"Where are the rest of the men?" Tekun asked.

"Dead. There was too many of them. You can only see them when they set heaven afire or swarm you." The man fell to his knees.

A servant knocked on the door.

"What is it?" Oba Bode asked.

"There's someone…" The woman started as she

entered.

"Speak up!" Tekun ordered.

"There's someone here to see the oba." The woman spoke as she looked at the floor.

"I'm not expecting anyone." Oba Bode looked at her confused.

"She says it's urgent. She says she has information about the Eje Okunrin."

"Send her." Oba Bode walked over to Tekun. "Get the men ready. I don't think we have much time. Send them to the west. They should be coming from there since they're traveling from the coast," he told a guard in the room. The guard exited to fulfill his orders.

Tekun turned to walk away but stopped when he saw a short beautiful dark skinned woman walking with a hooded cape. She revealed herself as she entered further into the room. The two men on her left and right did not.

"Announce yourself!" Tekun commanded.

"I am Fasina Odeyan. I come with news. I was

traveling along the trail to the city and stopped at the river to rest. I saw a militia of men crossing the river in boats."

The man on the floor raised his eyes to look at the woman speaking. "Oba, she's with them. She's his whore," the man shouted.

"Do you know of Sakin? The leader of the Eje Okunrin."

"I know the leader of the Blood Men. He's here right now."

The man on her left stabbed Tekun's chest with his machete. Ade was relieve when she noticed it was a warrior from her home village.

"Sakin!" Amoyi jumped out of his seat when the leopard slayer uncloaked himself and revealed a doubled headed ax in each hand.

Oba Bode looked at the boy with a sting in his heart. Amoyi never addressed him with such admiration or smiled at any of his accomplishments.

"How do you know this man?" he questioned Amoyi.

"He was at the Owura village. He taught me how to fight."

Ade grabbed Amoyi and held him close to her body.

Oba Bode laughed. He scratched his beard as his belly trembled. "That's why you've been so sweet," he said to Ade. He grabbed his paring knife and scratched the side of his face. He walked to Ade sideways with an eye still on his brother.

"Let them go, Bode. It's over." Sakin tried to reason as he walked forward.

"All this time I thought I got rid of you, the golden child. I thought I destroyed you and took everything you loved. But, right beneath my eyes you've live here in my own house." He looked at the boy. As he got closer Ade positioned herself in front of Amoyi. "Tonight this ends." Oba Bode lunged for Ade. She pushed Amoyi away as Bode grabbed her and wrapped his arm around her and put his knife to her throat.

Sakin hurried forward but stopped when he saw droplets of blood.

"I see you never stopped loving her." Oba Bode smiled wickedly. "I know why. She feels good. Even better when I forced her."

"Let her go."

"No, you will let me go and I will meet you on the battlefield." Oba Bode eased his way around the room, along the walls to the door.

Sakin and the others watched. When Fasina or the Jembe warrior tried to make a move Sakin halted them. Oba Bode ran out the door with Ade as Tekun rushed the Jembe man for distraction.

"Go after them. I'll take care of him," the Jembe man said as he wrestled with Tekun who was already weak from blood loss.

"Take my son and protect him," Sakin ordered Fasina before he ran after his brother.

Ade dug her heels into the ground. Oba Bode tripped her then dragged her by her hair. At the aafin entrance she bit his hand. He wanted to take her life but he ran out the door because there was no time.

"Ęlęwa," Sakin said as he knelt beside her.

"Go!" Ade pushed him out the door. "I'll be fine."
Oba Bode mounted his horse and met his warriors who were ready to head west to the coast. Along
the way he ordered a troop to go south. Sakin was behind him. Sakin heard his drummers setting everybody
in place. The sky turned gray. The clouds rumbled.
Sakin looked around and saw his brother heading west.
He mounted a horse and pursued his brother.

The villagers hurried to their houses. If their
house was too far away they pleaded to stay at another's
place. They didn't know what to expect. There had never been an attack in Jefe before. Ade found Fasina and
Amoyi inside the room where Tekun laid dead from
a broken neck. She told Amoyi to go hid in the secret
chambers in the basement. Outside she found a horse
in the compound and galloped through the streets of
Jefe informing the citizens.

"Omoba Sakin has risen from the dead!" she
shouted. "He comes to set you free from the monster
we call oba!"

On his way to the basement, Amoyi met Mofeyisade. She stood in the hall with a knife.

"I've been waiting for a moment like this," Mofeyisade said as Amoyi ran closer.

Behind him was Fasina with her machete. Mofeyisade lunged for Amoyi. Fasina cut Mofeyisade's arm with the machete. She dropped the knife. As Mofeyisade bent over to pick up the knife Fasina kicked her face. Mofeyisade fell backwards. When she turned around she grabbed Amoyi. She wrapped her hands around his neck. Amoyi struggled to find the knife on the floor near him. He watched Mofeyisade's face grimace as he plunged the knife into her side. She gasped as she fell back.

"Go!" Fasina yelled to Amoyi who sat in disbelief rubbing his neck. Fasina picked him up and continued to run down the stairs leaving Mofeyisade to die.

When the Jefe militia reached the south, Doye was ready with his men. Flaming arrows rained from atop the hill. Rows of men fell to the arrows with their horses. The rows of archers rotated until Doye commanded otherwise. Men kept storming uphill. Out the corner of Doye's eye he saw a red, green, and black cloth appear. It was Egungun. It danced in circles with its machetes out. Egungun jumped into the air with its cloth fluttering like kite tails and rolled down the hill cutting off the legs of any horse they came in contact with, sending the rider into the air. Doye ordered his men to charge.

Ibons were fired but the Eje Okunrin kept coming. If they were hit the bullets were crushed against their shields. Jefe militia men were grabbed from their horses and jabbed with spears or sliced by machetes. Some of the Eje Okunrin mounted the horses of the slain and continued their onslaught.

Tose waited in the field. He felt the earth tremble beneath him as Jefe warriors approached on their horses. He remembered every battle he fought by his son's side. Today, he thought he might not make it. He looked to his right at the long line of men with their faces painted red and white like the shields they carried. He looked to his left and saw the same. He returned his gaze to the middle of the field amazed to see his sons waiting. The Egungun with six arms of machetes danced with the others. The doom and void he felt dissipate. Today, there was no defeat planned for him. Today, he was a victor.

As the horsemen continued, the Egungun began spinning rapidly like a tornado. It created a vortex cutting the procession down the line, sucking up the men nearby. The Eje Okunrin watched in wonder. When the vortex slowed down Tose ordered his men to engage. They ran. They clashed with the horsemen throwing their spears into the rider's chests knocking them down.

It looked like a tidal wave swallowing his men as Oba Bode rode into the field. He saw many of them retreating from the field and from the hill. Many surrendered when they felt they could no longer run.

Oba Bode turned his horse around and rode back to Jefe. He saw Sakin. Lightning ripped the sky. Rain poured. When Oba Bode reached the village market Sakin was on his heels. Sakin jumped from his horse and knocked Oba Bode to the ground.

They tumbled knocking over box stands and tables. As they rolled Sakin released and rolled onto his feet and hands like a cat then stood up. Bode rose to his feet. He picked up a pointed wooden stick and threw it at Sakin like a spear. Sakin evaded it but by the time he regained his composure his brother punched him in the face. Oba Bode jammed his fists into Sakin's body repeatedly. Sakin tried to get away. Oba Bode grabbed Sakin's shoulders and brought Sakin's face to his knee. He knocked Sakin down and kicked him. Oba Bode then picked Sakin up and threw him into market stands.

Ade had galloped into the market. She unmounted her horse by Sakin's horse where his axes were tied. Doye, Tose and many others arrived forming a circle around the bothers. Doye wanted to help Sakin fight. Tose held him back.

"You're weak!" Bode shouted as Sakin tried to get up. "Is this who you want for your king?" he asked the spectators. "This is the man you love?" he said to Ade. "You're weak just like baba," he said when he returned to Sakin.

Ade unfastened Sakin's ax from the horse. It was almost too heavy for her. She threw it to Sakin. The ax slipped out of her hands and fell short. Sakin got up slowly. Oba Bode took large steps towards him. As his brother approached Sakin rolled to his side to evade him.

"You can't defeat me. I'm a god," Oba Bode said as he cracked his own neck by tilting it side to side.

When he got up Oba Bode punched Sakin's chest. Sakin flew backwards and hit the ground. Oba Bode walked to a warrior and ripped the machete from his waist. He went back to Sakin and rose the machete in the air. Tose tossed his machete to Sakin. He caught it. He met Bode mid air. As he rose, he pushed Bode's machete aside and kicked him in the chest. Sakin jumped into the air and punched his brother's forehead. Sakin cut Bode's thigh with the machete as he landed. Bode didn't bleed.

Bode recovered and charged at Sakin. As Sakin spun out of the way Bode slashed his back. Sakin groaned with pain. He grabbed Bode's left shoulder. As his hand slipped, his fingers caught Bode's charm. It was ripped by Sakin's fingertips as Bode pushed him away.

Ade unraveled the other ax and shouted for Sakin to catch. Doye grabbed it from her and towards Sakin flung it towards Sakin. He turned around and reached for it. Bode watched the double headed ax make its way to Sakin's hand. Sparks flew from the machete and ax when Bode tried to strike Sakin. He threw a punch but Sakin leaned back in time. Sakin returned with a punch of his own hitting Bode's jaw. Then Sakin kneed his stomach. Bode took a few steps back.

The heavens thundered as Sakin jumped in the air spun around with the ax. The ax's blade penetrated Bode's chest. Bode grunted, his face surprised. Blood spilled around the blade. The blade slipped out and pierced his chest again. Blood spurted from Bode's mouth as he took a few steps back while holding his chest. His knees weakened. He fell to his knees.

The roar of Sakin's agony thundered from his belly. As he screamed with the timber of a drum, lightning ripped through every gray cloud in the sky. The thunder God, pounded his heavenly drum letting Sakin know he supported him.

Clouds parted by yellow beams of sunlight from the east touched the earth. The ground drank Bode's blood as his wretched body laid.

Ade walked carefully towards Sakin. She gently place her hand over his double headed ax. His bloody grip loosened, releasing the ax that buried its blade into the wet earth. Ade lifted his chin with the curve of her index finger, lightly wiping the blood on his face with the palm of her hand. She wanted to take the pain away, his sorrow, carry it for him. If she could sacrifice a ten thousand rams to do so she would. However, she knew fate was never hers to decide.

"The kingdom of Jefe awaits you, Oba Sakin."

Sakin tuned to view his subjects, those who were loyal, the surviving subjects who fought with his brother against him along with the citizens who came out of hiding to witness this epic war they'll recite to their offspring. All prostrated before him.

The sun rays warmed Sakin's skin. "The Deities smile upon our kingdom again because of you," Ade said as she bowed her head and stepped backwards.

"May the Gods and Goddesses bless our kingdom as the day dawns upon your new king! Oba Sakin Adesine. Son of Oba Kola Adesine, descendant of the Thunder God himself!" He lifted his ax from the earth and jolted it in the air. "Kawo Kabiesi!" His voice met the thunder of the heavens.

"Kawo Kabiesi!" Everyone hailed the Sky God in return.

Iyalase, who observed everything from a nearby tree, approvingly nodded then flew back into the heavens. Along the way she picked up the charm Bode wore and swallowed it whole so that no living soul should come across it. She smiled. Balance was restored.

A split calabash can be mended.

One who spits fire burns everything.

One who is patient gets to the end of a troubling road.

Cast for Oba Kola who was told his kingdom would split into two. The Thunder God would make sure it becomes one again. And that is would swell. Do not worry, the kingdom will become one again.

Glossay/Phrases

*unless noted otherwise many of the words are
of Yoruba origin

Aafin Palace

Abami Monster

Adahunṡe A person skilled at making magic

Adupe Thank you

Agan A ritual clothing animated by the Ancestors and
is treated as a shrine.

Ago Excuse Me

Alagbara Strong

Alagbede A Blacksmith

Arèmo Prince to become king

Assegias A slender, iron tipped hardwood spear

Ayaba Queen

Ayo A popular game of strategy indigenous to Africa

Baba Father

Babalawo Father of secrets. A male priest initiated to
Ifa. This priest may divine to let a person know more
in depth about their past, future and present.

Bawo ni? How are you?

Beeni Yes

Binrin Princess

Buba A dashiki

Cowrie A marine mollusk that's smooth, glossy and domed traditionally used as money and decoration

Da Good

Dide Rise, get up

Ebo Sacrifice, offering

Eje Okunrin Blood Men

Elẹwa Beautiful

Emi ni I am

Emir Sultan/ King, a title used by the Turegs.

Eniyan People

Epo Palm Oil

Essien *(Ga/Ochi/Nigerian/Ibibio/Efik)* Sixth Born or belongs to everyone

Ẹso Royal Guard

Fila hat

Gbogbo epere All is better

Gele A head wrap or dressing for women

Ibon Gun

Igbo Forest

Ile House

Iya Mother

Iya Oba Queen Mother

Iyawo Wife

Jakuta An african style of martial arts

Jojolo A ritual song sang asking the mother of the newborn to come and show the baby to everyone.

Jowol Please

Kaftan A dress worn by women in the Tureg tradition.

Kora An African musical instrument, ancestor of the guitar. It has 21 strings placed on a gourd and is covered with animal skin.

Lapa A wrap around skirt

Marimba A musical instrument, ancestor to the xylophone created by the goddess Marimba, the mother of music, happiness and tribal singers.

Ma se gbe Stop it

Mi My

Mo ni fe I love you

Nyanga A west African windpipe instrument

Oba King

Obi Leader of a village

Obinrin Woman

Ode A passage from the odus within Ifa

Odu Spiritual messenges within Ifa that speaks about various situations

Olori Chief

Omi Water

Omo Child

Omoba A prince

Opele A divining tool of a babalawo

Ore mi My friend

Ori Shea Butter

Oyin Honey

Saber A sword that has a wide blade and a curved point

Se alafia ni "I am well." *(A widely used response to "How are you?")*

Shekere An instrument made from a dried gourd covered with beads

Tani se? Who are you?

Wá Come

Yuvo White man

African Divinities

Egungun- The collective of all the matriarchs and patriarchs of the family that continue to take of the family needs.

Elegba- The divinity of communication. He carries out the will of Oludumare. He sits at all crossroads. His number is three and his colors are red and black.

Ifa -A divinity, also known as Orunmilla, and an ancient cultural system. He is second only to Olodumare. His colors are green and yellow. He knows the beginning to the end of everything.

Íyami- The sacred mothers that govern everything in the universe. They are represented by birds, especially vultures. Their colors are red, black and white.

Obaluaiye- The divinity of the earth who not only spreads disease but cures it. He is hot and cool at the same time. His number is seventeen and some of his many colors are black, white and purple.

Ogun- A warrior divinity governing war and is Iron itself. His number is seven and his colors are green, black and red.

Olódùmarè- The supreme creator of the universe from which everything extends.

Orisha Oko - The divinity of the farm and the process of changing from one position in   life to another. His colors are red and white.

Osun- The divinity of love and culture. She makes things that are hard to deal with easy. She is the wife of Orunmilla. Her colors are yellow, honey and orange.

Oya- A warrior divinity governing the dead transition, the marketplace and change. She is the wife of Sango. Her number is nine and some of her colors are purple and maroon.

Sango A sky divinity governing kingship, justice and male fertility. His number is six and his colors are red and white.

Towiyo The Ancestral heads of a lineage that sits closest to the Gods.

Oriki

(praise poems)

Oriki Osun

Osun mo me o o.

Olomodi mo me o.

Ololodi mo me o.

Mo pe o sowo.

Mo pe o somo.

Mo pe o si aiku.

Mo pe o si oro.

Eniti nwa omo ko fun lomo.

Emi ko fe odi,

Emi ko fe aro.

Omo daradara ni ki fun won.

Oriki Sango

Egun ara oyo

Ara ewo ara ede

Omo odo oba

Ti ó ba nse

Won a ma a sóre' kiri

Won a ní ịtale ló nja wón

Oníle ori okè fiti

Isale ká mi mo

Ti wón ba pe Oya

Ko dáhún ni ile irá

Ti wón ba pe ori

About The Author

Oyabiyi Ajinaku is a Chicago native that currently resides in Phoenix. One of her earliest memories of telling stories is giving her handwritten novels to her cousins and friends to read. She pursued creative writing at Columbia College Chicago. She eventually settled on pursuing enterprenuership and real estate while she writes full time.

Oyabiyi has a wonderful son who she cares for and lots of family and friends she enjoys spending time with over a good home cooked meal. When she is not writing, Oyabiyi is trying a new recipe, creating content for her media company and figuring out how to garden in the desert.

Her future goals include creating a travel writing group to help others self-publish their books. She also plans to turn her novels and short stories into film so that her messages reach a larger audience.

To stay in the loop be sure to join her newsletter at
www.oyabiyiajinaku.com

www.ingramcontent.com/pod-product-compliance
Lightning Source LLC
Chambersburg PA
CBHW060421030726
47495CB00003B/684